# "Why do you wear those glasses?" Griffin asked.

"Um...so I can see?"

"You used to wear contacts. Those pictures in the living room—no glasses."

"Very observant of you." Raleigh shrugged. "Glasses are less trouble, and they make me look smarter. That helps in the courtroom."

"They're also easy to hide behind. You go to a lot of trouble to make sure men don't notice you."

"Is that any of your business?" she asked sharply.

"Maybe not. But reporters are naturally curious. Other men might not look past the frumpy lawyer facade, but I have. You're a beautiful woman, Raleigh. Why don't you let the world see that?"

As he'd spoken, her eyes had grown wide. But she didn't deny anything. The anger he saw reflected in her expression gradually receded, replaced by a look of perplexity.

Griffin touched her chin with one forefinger, leaned forward, and did what he'd been thinking about since walking through the front door.

Dear Reader,

In the 1970s, the whole country became fascinated
with the investigative reporting of Woodward and
Bernstein, whose Watergate stories brought down a
president. Journalism became a popular major for
college students, including me. Alas, I was never
hard-hitting enough to be a good investigative
reporter. The best I could come up with was a
story about two competing pizza restaurants titled
(cleverly, I thought) Pizza Wars.

But the fun thing about being a novelist is
that I get to be any kind of person through my
characters. Griffin Benedict is the tough but
compassionate journalist I wanted to be, jetting
off to war zones and natural disasters, shining the
light of truth into shady dealings. And who better
for him to investigate than upstanding, uptight
Project Justice attorney Raleigh Shinn, who has
never so much as been late with a library book?

I had a great deal of fun pitting these two smart
yet very different people against each other, then
forcing them to team up to face the real threat. I
hope you enjoy it.

Sincerely,

Kara Lennox

# Nothing But the Truth
## *Kara Lennox*

TORONTO  NEW YORK  LONDON
AMSTERDAM  PARIS  SYDNEY  HAMBURG
STOCKHOLM  ATHENS  TOKYO  MILAN  MADRID
PRAGUE  WARSAW  BUDAPEST  AUCKLAND

Recycling programs
for this product may
not exist in your area.

ISBN-13: 978-0-373-71695-1

NOTHING BUT THE TRUTH

# ABOUT THE AUTHOR

Kara Lennox has earned her living at various times as an art director, typesetter, textbook editor and reporter. She's worked in a boutique, a health club and an ad agency. She's been an antiques dealer, an artist and even a blackjack dealer. But no work has ever made her happier than writing romance novels. To date, she has written more than sixty books. Kara is a recent transplant to Southern California. When not writing, she indulges in an ever-changing array of hobbies. Her latest passions are bird-watching, long-distance bicycling, vintage jewelry and, by necessity, do-it-yourself home renovation. She loves to hear from readers; you can find her at www.karalennox.com.

**Books by Kara Lennox**

**HARLEQUIN SUPERROMANCE**
1689—TAKEN TO THE EDGE††

**HARLEQUIN AMERICAN ROMANCE**
974—FORTUNE'S TWINS
990—THE MILLIONAIRE NEXT DOOR
1052—THE FORGOTTEN COWBOY
1068—HOMETOWN HONEY*
1081—DOWNTOWN DEBUTANTE*
1093—OUT OF TOWN BRIDE*
1146—THE FAMILY RESCUE**
1150—HER PERFECT HERO**
1154—AN HONORABLE MAN**
1180—ONE STUBBORN TEXAN
1195—GOOD HUSBAND MATERIAL
1216—RELUCTANT PARTNERS†
1240—THE PREGNANCY SURPRISE†
1256—THE GOOD FATHER†

††Project Justice
*Blond Justice
**Firehouse 59
†Second Sons

Believe it or not, this one's
for my ex-husband, Pete, who really did
jet off to war zones and natural disasters
with his trusty Nikon. I'm still in awe
of the danger you put yourself in,
and the beautiful pictures you took.

## CHAPTER ONE

RALEIGH SHINN HESITATED on the sidewalk outside the coffee shop, her palms damp, her chest tight. She hadn't been this nervous since she'd argued a case before the Texas Supreme Court.

She so much preferred to be the one asking the questions. But she had committed to the interview; she couldn't weasel out.

Raleigh did not like the media. Even when she fought for a popular cause, the press often described her as a bulldog, a terrier, or a sexless, humorless legal machine.

Those descriptions were, perhaps, not entirely undeserved. But now, she needed some good press, because her current cause was decidedly unpopular. It would take a tidal wave of evidence to get the D.A. to reopen the case of Anthony Simonetti, currently sitting on death row for supposedly gunning down his girlfriend in a cold-blooded act of premeditation. Raleigh wanted public sentiment squarely on her side when she made her argument.

Griffin Benedict, roving investigative reporter for the *Houston Telegram,* could turn public opinion. He was immensely popular—almost a celebrity in his own right. People believed what he wrote. He could help her cause.

Or he could crucify her. She had to take her chances.

After a deep, fortifying breath, she entered Legal Grounds, a coffee shop near the Harris County Courthouse.

She spotted him immediately. Even if she hadn't seen his picture, she would have known he was the one. He was the only man sitting alone, and he was staring right at her.

Lord have mercy, he was gorgeous.

That thought surprised her. She didn't normally think of men in terms of their looks. She sometimes sized up a client's appearance and how it would play with a judge or jury, but she couldn't remember the last time she had found a man attractive.

Griffin Benedict's sexual magnetism hit her like a fog bank, momentarily disorienting her. Brown hair, longish and with a rakish wave, framed a square-jawed, tanned face. The nose had a slight bump, as if it had been broken. Mouth, sensual. That was the adjective that leaped to mind, although she wasn't sure what made it so.

His broad shoulders filled out a button-down shirt rolled up to the elbows, open at the throat, tucked into well-worn jeans. Scuffed cowboy boots, of course.

He continued to stare at her, frowning slightly, and she shook herself out of her stupor. *Eyes forward, posture erect.* She had to show quiet confidence. She strode forward, hand outstretched.

"Mr. Benedict."

He stood and flashed a welcoming smile, his large hand swallowing hers before giving it a firm shake. Either his hand was very warm, or hers was cold. Would he note that? Would he attribute her lack of circulation to nerves? Although it was late September, the weather was still warm, no reason for cold hands.

"Ms. Shinn. Good to meet you. Would you like something to drink? I was just going to get myself a coffee."

"No, thank you."

"Be right back, then."

He was tall, well over six feet. She was five-nine, and she wore heels, so she didn't often look up to people. She watched him walk up to the counter with an easy saunter and then tore her eyes away when she realized she'd focused too long on the way his backside filled out those faded jeans.

Maybe she should have ordered hot tea. It would give her something to do with her hands. But her choice of drink revealed something about her psyche, and she wanted to avoid that. This interview was about her work.

When Benedict returned to the table, he held two steaming cups.

"You must be very thirsty," she said.

"The tea is for you. In case you change your mind."

Raleigh's whole body tingled. How had he known hot tea would be her beverage of choice? Lucky guess? She did not like his presumptive gesture, but she chose not to let him know of her irritation. He might be trying to get a rise out of her.

She firmly set the tea aside, though, perversely, it did tempt her. Darjeeling, her favorite. *How could he know?*

It would have been prudent for her to do a more thorough background check on Griffin Benedict. She felt distinctly uncomfortable, knowing he had done some digging around of his own. He apparently had learned more than her win/loss record in court.

"I know you're busy." He pulled a reporter's notebook from his breast pocket. "So we'll get right to work. You don't mind this, do you?" He set a digital recorder in the center of the table.

"No, of course not." She had no reason to fear the recorder. She wouldn't make any verbal missteps, and the recording might protect her from being misquoted.

"First, congratulations on your victory in the Eldon Jasperson case."

"Thank you, but the victory belongs to everyone at Project Justice. It was a group effort. All I did was file papers."

"Modest. I like that." He smiled, revealing his blindingly white teeth, and she noticed his eyes for the first time. They were a deep, sincere brown. He had probably disarmed any number of female interviewees with that smile and those eyes.

She couldn't deny a certain awareness of him as a man, but she was pretty sure she wouldn't show it. She met his gaze squarely and gave him a reserved smile, waiting for him to continue.

"Yes, well, let's move on to the Anthony Simonetti case. Another death row inmate. In fact, most of your cases are for prisoners on death row, correct?"

"Project Justice is normally the defense of last resort. We deal with the most serious, the most urgent cases, many of which are capital crime convictions." Raleigh relaxed slightly. Now they were in comfortable territory for her.

"So you believe Anthony Simonetti is innocent?" he asked with an obvious note of cynicism.

"An important piece of evidence has surfaced, which might exonerate Anthony," she said, using her client's first name in the hopes of distancing him from his infamous mobster father. Leo Simonetti was rumored to have beheaded one of his enemies with a machete.

"But do *you* believe the man is innocent? I mean, come on. He was picked up two blocks from the crime scene, covered with his dead girlfriend's blood. He claims he happened upon Michelle Brewster moments after her murder, and that was how he got her blood on him. But wouldn't an innocent man have then summoned the authorities? Instead of fleeing?"

Benedict had keyed in on the most damning evidence against Anthony. "He was overcome with shock and grief. He fled from the horror of what he had just discovered. No, he did not behave logically. Many people, in a crisis, do not behave logically."

She knew this for a fact. She had walked away from the car accident that had killed her husband. Uninjured, but covered with his blood, she had fled the car and wandered along the icy road in her inadequate coat and shoes until the police had spotted her and picked her up. She'd been dazed, incoherent. To this day, she had no memory of the accident, or the few minutes before and after.

"So you do believe he's innocent."

She suppressed all thoughts of Jason, which could swamp her in grief at a moment's notice. Sudden tears were not something she relished explaining to a reporter.

"I believe only in what the evidence tells me. Additional evidence has been found, and it has something to say."

"The district attorney has said he will not reopen the case, that the right man is behind bars."

"District attorneys seldom admit to mistakes— especially around election time."

"So you think Simonetti didn't get a fair trial?"

"That's not the issue. I believe the D.A. did the

proper thing at the time, given the evidence presented."

"And what about now?"

"I don't agree with the police department's decision to ignore the gun that was recently found in the water heater next door to the crime scene—especially since finding the murder weapon is the one thing that could prove someone else was involved in the crime."

"I understand that the gun is corroded. It can't even be test fired, and the serial number is unreadable."

How did he know that? Since the gun's discovery had already appeared on the news, Project Justice had sent out a carefully worded press release regarding the foundation's plans to find out if the gun was significant to Michelle Brewster's murder. The release hadn't mentioned anything about severe corrosion.

She smiled, saying nothing.

"And even if testing were possible," Benedict continued, "aren't you afraid it would put the last nail in Anthony's coffin? That could prove embarrassing for Project Justice."

The reporter had quickly homed in on the weakest point of her case. As he fled the scene, Anthony himself could have hidden the gun inside the neighbor's water heater, which was easily accessible.

"I can't comment as to the specifics of the case," Raleigh said, stepping back onto her comfortable platform. She preferred that her arguments be presented first to a judge—not debated in the media.

"You always say that when you don't like the direction an interview is taking." Benedict leaned forward, too close for comfort. "I've read every news story in which you were quoted, watched every bit of available video in which you were interviewed. When a hard question is asked, you suddenly can't comment."

She tried not to show how much his intensity rattled her. Tough reporters had gone after her before. She was used to it. This was nothing compared to what she'd faced when filing motions on behalf of Eldon Jasperson, a convicted child murderer.

So why did it bother her so much? Why did *this* reporter bother her so much?

"Difficult questions usually involve the specifics of an ongoing case, which I cannot discuss. No mystery about that."

"I would argue that the Simonetti case is different. It seems…out of character for you. You normally don't take on cases without more compelling evidence."

"Each case presented to Project Justice is evaluated based on a unique set of circumstances. We felt this case had merit." Granted, it had been a hard sell to Daniel Logan, Project Justice's founder and the ultimate decision maker. If the gun could be traced back to Anthony or anyone in his extensive criminal family, the foundation would be inundated with negative publicity, which tended to cause donations and sponsors to dry up.

But Raleigh believed in Anthony's truthfulness when he told her he did not own—had never owned—a gun. She had even taken the extra precaution of recording her interview with Anthony on video, then having Claudia Ellison, the foundation's on-call psychologist, evaluate Anthony's demeanor. An expert on body language, Claudia had found no sign of deceit. Daniel trusted Raleigh's and Claudia's instincts.

If Raleigh was wrong about this one, her reputation would take a hard blow. But she felt strongly enough to take the risk.

"I don't believe you," Griffin said, startling her. "Do you want to know why?"

"I feel certain you're going to enlighten me," she said with a smugness she didn't truly feel. Suddenly Griffin Benedict seemed dangerous.

She took a sip of her tea, despite her earlier decision not to drink it. It was easier to hide her emotions behind a paper cup and her steamed-up glasses.

"I have reliable information that you, personally, received incentives to convince the Project Justice decision makers to take on Anthony's case. Specifically, that you accepted a bribe."

Raleigh set her cup down with a thud, splashing tea everywhere. "What? Are you crazy?" Who would tell a reporter such a thing about her? Or had he made it up, trying to shake her composure?

Damn it, he'd succeeded. A few nearby coffee-shop patrons looked over curiously.

*Don't make a scene, Raleigh.* She could hear her mother-in-law's voice in her ear, trying to hush Raleigh when she'd been out of her mind with grief. Back then, she had let her big, sloppy emotions spill out onto everyone in her path—cops, doctors, reporters, many of whom blamed her for her husband's death.

She had learned self-control since then.

"I'm just telling you what I heard." Griffin took another sip of his coffee.

Raleigh scooted her chair back. "I hadn't realized this was going to be a character assassination instead of an interview. Please don't call me again." She reached for her briefcase on the floor by her chair, intending to make a dramatic exit.

"Wait."

His single word froze her to her seat. She wished she could have ignored him. But he was so damn compelling.

"I didn't just take someone's word for it. I demanded proof—and I got this." He extended a piece of paper across the table toward her. "Does this look familiar?"

Raleigh grew dizzy as every drop of blood in her body fell to her feet. Yes, the paper did look familiar.

It was a copy of her bank statement. The one that showed a twenty-thousand-dollar deposit made to her account from a numbered Swiss bank account.

She should have known. She had tried to tell the bank that the deposit was in error, but they'd insisted it wasn't. Then she had become frantically busy. She had pushed all thoughts of the aberrant deposit out of her mind, figured someone, somewhere, would miss their money, and the error would be corrected.

"Care to explain the rather large chunk of change that landed in your account?"

"No, I would not," Raleigh said succinctly, trying not to panic. "Would *you* care to explain how you came to be in possession of my private financial information? Because I'm pretty sure there's an invasion-of-privacy issue here. I could sue you up one side and down the other."

"But you won't. Because you wouldn't want this little piece of paper to become a matter of public record, would you?"

He was right about that.

"Don't worry, Raleigh—may I call you Raleigh?"

She refused to answer.

"I'm not going to publish the specifics of your bank account. But I do intend to find out what's going on with you. If there is an innocent explanation for the deposit, set me straight."

"There is, but it's none of your business. If you want to investigate me, knock yourself out. I have never accepted payment beyond my salary for the work I do at Project Justice, and I never will."

On that note, she made her exit. She could have sworn she felt Griffin Benedict's eyes burning into her back as she walked out the door.

GRIFFIN CLICKED off his recorder, watching as the auburn-haired ice queen glided out the door.

That had gone about as expected. Someone with Raleigh Shinn's experience in high-pressure legal situations wouldn't cave in and confess with his first salvo.

*She* wasn't what he expected, though. Of course he'd seen pictures and video of her. He'd thought she was plain, even somewhat unattractive in her clunky glasses, boxy man suits and hair slicked back into a matronly bun.

But in person, she was something entirely different. For one thing, she had a figure underneath those suits. He'd seen the hint of generous breasts beneath her jacket when she had reached for her tea, the barest shadow of cleavage above the top button of her cream silk shirt.

Her hair wasn't a boring brown, as he'd believed, but had threads of fiery red and gold mixed in. Her real color, too. If she'd had even a day's worth of roots, he'd have spotted it.

She apparently wore no makeup, but her skin was

a translucent ivory, smooth and soft-looking. And she had a dusting of freckles across her nose.

Nice mouth. Kissable.

But her eyes had intrigued him the most. Those scholarly horn-rim glasses hid eyes of a deep, emerald green with gold flecks. In them he saw flashes of fire, especially when she talked about her work.

She wore a wedding ring, he'd noted, but she wasn't married. Her husband had died six years ago. Maybe she wore the ring as yet more protection. Practically everything about her screamed that she was unavailable, not an object to be desired or lusted after by men.

Her strategy had the opposite effect on him. He had always been intrigued by the librarian types. Uptight clothes, glasses, frosty demeanor—those were traits that gave his libido a wake-up call. He was curious to learn more about what was beneath the shapeless clothes, and he fantasized about pulling off the glasses, mussing the neat hair.…

Hell, what was he doing? Raleigh Shinn wasn't a potential lover. She was a sanctimonious lawyer who might or might not be guilty of accepting a bribe to use her influence unfairly.

Many convicts pleaded their cases to Project Justice. From what Griffin had heard, the foundation considered all of them, but took on only a very few.

Had Anthony Simonetti—or his wealthy, criminal

father—leapfrogged over other, more worthy cases with the help of some green incentive?

The jury was still out. Griffin had received only an anonymous tip about Raleigh, plus the copy of her bank statement left under the windshield wiper of his car. He did not yet have enough solid information to go to print, nor even enough to form his own opinion. The current facts as he knew them would not impress the network that was considering him for an anchor position on a national TV news magazine.

But the potential for an exciting story was there. Project Justice was hot news right now, and Raleigh's possible criminal actions could explode in the foundation's face, making for a splashy, TV-worthy, journalistic tour de force.

But first, he had to learn more. He wanted to know everything there was to know about Raleigh Shinn. Mostly, he wanted to know why she hid a hot body and a beautiful face behind that dumpy facade.

# CHAPTER TWO

"BUT IT HAS to be a mistake." Raleigh had been on the phone for twenty-two minutes, first on hold, then working her way up the corporate ladder of Houston Federal Bank. She was now talking to a vice president.

"If it was a mistake," the condescending man said, "it wasn't on our end. Now, it's possible whoever made the deposit mistyped a number."

"Exactly! So can't you just contact them and ask?"

"I'm afraid not. Numbered bank accounts are numbered for a reason. We've sent a query to the transmitting institution, but we haven't yet received a reply."

"So maybe you could just—send the money back."

"That's impossible. Where would we send it?"

"Then put it wherever you put unclaimed funds."

"I'm not sure why you're so upset, Ms. Shinn. If there was an error, it will be corrected in a day or two."

She considered telling him that the twenty thousand dollars sitting in her account was causing her all kinds of trouble. Then she decided on a different strategy. If she couldn't solve the mystery of the strange deposit, maybe she could find out how Griffin got a copy of her statement.

"Mr. Temple," she said, referring to the name she had jotted down. She kept detailed notes of every phone conversation. If her mother called to tell her she had a cold, Raleigh made a note and filed it.

"Yes, Ms. Shinn? Is there something else I can do for you?"

"How secure is your online banking? I mean, how hard would it be for someone to hack into your system?"

"I assure you, ma'am, our computers are hack-proof. Every transaction uses the latest in encryption technology."

"So there is absolutely no way someone could get access to my statement without my permission? What about bank personnel?"

"In most cases of illicit access to bank accounts, the security loophole lies with the client. Mail can be intercepted. A password can be stolen or, more often, divulged to someone who shouldn't have it."

She started to vehemently deny the problem could be on her end. She memorized her passwords, never wrote them down anywhere. But she did receive paper statements.

"Very well, thank you, Mr. Temple."

"My pleasure, Ms. Shinn."

She hung up, knowing little more than she'd known half an hour ago.

Given what Griffin Benedict had told her, she had to view that strange deposit with new eyes. Rather than a mistake, could it be part of a plot to ruin her? If someone really had provided Griffin with that bogus tip along with the stolen bank statement, it meant she had an enemy. A powerful one who had gone to some expense to wreck her reputation.

Plenty of people did not like her. The nature of her job was confrontational. She was constantly challenging unlawful judicial proceedings, inept lawyers, negligent police investigators. When a conviction was overturned, it meant someone, somewhere, had made a mistake or worse, and she had brought it to light.

Some of her own clients didn't even like her. Few of them were shining examples of virtue.

Then there was the general public. Project Justice received hate mail all the time from people who thought the foundation's mission was to let killers out on the street.

The press alternated between loving her and hating her. She'd been in the news a lot lately with the Eldon Jasperson thing.

Even her own in-laws despised her. She'd never shared a warm relationship with them: they hadn't considered her a good match for their only son. Once they'd realized they couldn't talk Jason out of the wedding, they had tolerated her. But after Jason's death, the claws had come out again.

Jason's parents had blamed her for the fatal car accident. As if she hadn't heaped enough guilt onto herself.

After his funeral, she had quickly learned of her perilous financial situation. Everything Jason had owned was in trust, controlled by his parents, and they weren't inclined to give her a dime. Without him and his family's financial support, she could not continue running the law practice she and her husband had poured all of their passion into.

Their small firm of Shinn & Shinn had specialized in providing solid legal representation to those who couldn't afford to pay exorbitant legal fees—and they'd never made a profit. All of their living expenses had been drawn from Jason's trust. If Project Justice hadn't come along at the right time, Raleigh would have had to accept her only other job offer, as a drone at a corporate law firm.

Raleigh's stomach growled, reminding her she hadn't had lunch. Daniel kept the office kitchen stocked with all kinds of healthy goodies, but Raleigh needed fresh air. A walk around the corner to her favorite deli was in order.

As she passed through the lobby she walked on tiptoe, hoping to avoid the receptionist's attention. Celeste Boggs was one of the most terrifying people Raleigh knew. She was a vigilant watchdog, could purportedly shoot the wings off a gnat at fifty yards, and was fiercely loyal to Daniel Logan. Raleigh didn't doubt the seventy-something woman would lay down her life to protect the foundation.

But Celeste was short on manners, and once she started talking she was hard to walk away from. Right now, thankfully, she appeared to be engrossed in a copy of *True Romance.*

Raleigh had almost reached the revolving door when Celeste's screech of a voice rooted her to the spot.

"Ms. Shinn? Is that you?"

She turned, forcing a smile. "Yes. I was just—"

"You have to sign out. How many times do I have to tell you young people to sign in and out?"

"But I was just going to—"

Celeste extended the clipboard and pen toward Raleigh with an admonishing frown.

Fearing Celeste would give her detention if she argued further, Raleigh signed the sheet.

"I've been meaning to ask, where do you get your hair done?" Celeste asked.

"My hair?" No one ever asked her that. "I cut it myself. That's about all I do to it, besides wash it." Raleigh didn't have time for fancy salons. So long as her hair was out of her face and reasonably neat, she was happy.

"That explains it," Celeste murmured, pushing her purple glasses back onto the bridge of her nose.

Raleigh put a self-conscious hand up to her hair. Not that Celeste had a lot of room to criticize, with her wildly curly gray locks pointing every which way. But was Raleigh's do that bad?

She was about to turn back toward the door when Beth McClelland, Project Justice's physical evidence coordinator, rushed into the lobby, her platform shoes clattering noisily on the wood floor.

"Oh, Raleigh, I'm so glad I caught you."

Celeste frowned her disapproval at Beth. "Ms. Shinn is officially signed out. You'll have to wait until she gets back."

Raleigh wasn't about to ignore her best friend. "What is it, Beth?"

Beth shook a manila envelope triumphantly in the air. "I got the DNA results back on the Rhiner case," she said in a singsong voice. "And I think you're going to like the resu—"

"What part of *signed out* don't you understand?" Celeste interrupted.

"Just leave it on my desk," Raleigh said in a stage whisper to Beth. "My office door is open."

Celeste tsked.

Beth looked puzzled. "Are you okay? You don't look so good. I mean, normally you would be prying these DNA results out of my hands."

Raleigh brought herself back to the here and now. Beth was right—she should be excited. "So Rhiner didn't do it?"

"Not only that, but the FBI got a hit on their computer. New suspect. Next-door neighbor."

"Girls!" Celeste objected. "You're in a public place! You must discuss your sensitive information somewhere else."

Beth looked around at the otherwise deserted lobby, then hid a smile. "Sorry." She quickly signed out, then walked with Raleigh out the door.

"Where you off to?"

"Just the deli."

"I'll walk with you. Are you sure nothing's wrong?"

Beth's concern warmed Raleigh. She was the only real friend Raleigh had at work. Not that she didn't admire and respect her colleagues, but she kept a deliberate distance from them.

Except for Beth. When Beth had gone through an ugly breakup last year, Raleigh had found her crying in the ladies' room more than once, and her heart had gone out to the woman. She understood pain, and she had done what she could to make Beth feel better. Once Beth started confiding in Raleigh, Raleigh had naturally revealed more of herself.

Raleigh needed to tell someone of her current dilemma, but not in line at the deli counter.

"I'll tell you—when we can have a more private conversation."

"Uh-oh, this sounds bad."

Raleigh said nothing until she had her turkey-and-low-fat-mozzerella on whole wheat and had found an out-of-the-way table tucked into a corner.

"It's not a big deal," she finally said. "It's just that my bank made a mistake on my account, and it's causing me some trouble. Plus, there's a reporter who seems intent on publishing an unflattering story about me. I wouldn't care so much, except I don't want to make the foundation look bad."

"Oh, Raleigh, that's awful! About the reporter, I mean. Start with the bank, though. What did they do? Have they lost a deposit or something?"

"Just the opposite, actually." She explained to Beth about the anomalous twenty grand suddenly appearing on her balance sheet.

"Wow, that is so weird. I wish someone would make that kind of mistake in my account." Beth took a few sips of her banana smoothie. "Do you think it could be your in-laws? Maybe they're feeling guilty over the way they've treated you. To deliberately cut you off like that, when they knew good and well Jason would have wanted you taken care of—it just burns me up every time I think about it."

Raleigh had actually considered the possibility that her in-laws were involved somehow. Since they had most of Jason's papers—they had hired someone to clean out his office while she was at the funeral—they could be privy to Raleigh's financial information. But she hadn't spoken to them in over a year.

"It's unlikely they're involved." Raleigh took a

deep breath and told her the rest—about Griffin Benedict, and the fact he had a copy of her bank statement.

Beth was predictably incensed. "That's not just slimy, it's illegal. You're a lawyer, can't you…get him arrested? Sue him?"

"I can't. I don't want to bring negative publicity to the foundation, and I don't have time for a personal legal battle. I have too much work to do. Anyway, I don't want any more attention focused on me until I figure out what that deposit is all about."

"Why don't you talk to Mitch?" Beth suggested brightly. "He knows everything about computer hacking and identity theft. Maybe he can tell you how it was done."

Raleigh felt a ray of hope. "Beth, that's an excellent suggestion." Mitch Delacroix was Project Justice's tech expert. He had a background in cyber crime, a field he had entered after getting arrested as a teenager for hacking into a city government computer system in an attempt to fix a speeding ticket.

After dodging a felony conviction, he had decided to use his skills on the right side of the law. But he could still hack into anything, anywhere. And though no one on the staff was allowed to ask him to do anything illegal, Raleigh knew he often tiptoed around places in secure cyberspace where he didn't belong.

"We'll go talk to him as soon as you're done with lunch."

"I'm done now." She'd taken a few bites of the sandwich. That would be enough to keep her going. Beth led the way out of the deli, her brown corkscrew curls bouncing with every step of her wildly impractical pink platforms.

"I hate to use the foundation's resources for my own personal problems," Raleigh said.

"If you ask me, this *is* a Project Justice problem. If you get slammed with a negative story—and by Griffin Benedict, who has a kazillion readers—it'll hurt the foundation."

Maybe Beth was right.

Mitch could almost always be found in the bull pen. He had a private office on the second floor, two doors down from Raleigh's. The large, open bull pen downstairs was for junior investigators, interns and temporary workers. But since Mitch spent most of his time alone in cyberspace, he preferred to have the noise and activity of people around him in the physical world.

"You actually met Griffin Benedict face-to-face?" Beth asked as they quickly signed in while Celeste watched them over the top of her purple glasses with eagle eyes.

"I did."

"Is he as gorgeous as he looked in that magazine?" Beth led the way down the hallway toward the bull pen.

"What magazine?"

"You know. *Houston Scene*. They published the story about the ten most eligible bachelors in town."

This was news to Raleigh. She read the paper—and she often read Benedict's stories, which she had to admit were always riveting. "I had no idea he'd received such a *prestigious* distinction."

"Oh, yes. He made number three on the list, right behind Carl Black."

"Carl Black? Who is that?"

"Only the next major Hollywood heartthrob, from right here in our own backyard. Raleigh, where have you been?"

"Working, I guess." She didn't go to movies or watch much TV, and she definitely didn't keep up with celebrity gossip.

"You didn't answer my question. Drool-worthy?"

"It's hard to think of him in those terms, given that he's trying to ruin me," Raleigh lied through her teeth. He was the best-looking man she'd ever met. Or at least the sexiest.

*Sorry, Jason.*

She was certain she would never fall in love again. She'd met Jason at Princeton, in law school, and she'd fallen instantly—hard. But physical attraction hadn't brought them together. He'd been handsome enough, but he had bowled her over with his quiet intelligence and his commitment to ideals so similar to her own. She would never find that again.

Beth stopped in the hallway just before they entered the bull pen. "Do you ever feel that way about anyone? I mean, this place is testosterone city. We're hip-deep in good-looking men, many of them unattached, and you seem immune."

True, until recently. After Jason, she'd never looked at another man and gotten that zany, heart-flipping feeling. Then Griffin Benedict had come on the scene.

"I'm just not interested in making that connection again, Beth." That much was true.

Beth blushed. "I guess that was kind of a rude question. But sometimes I wish I could be detached like you, instead of wearing my heart on my sleeve all the time."

It might have been a rude question from someone else, but not from Beth. Raleigh knew she cared about her.

She smiled at Beth. "It's okay."

Raleigh wasn't sure she liked being described as "detached." Lawyers weren't supposed to get emotionally involved in their cases. But that word, *detached,* that was how she thought of her in-laws.

Mitch Delacroix hunched over his keyboard in his usual corner, peering at the screen through the special glasses he wore for computer work. As always, it took Beth some effort to get Mitch's attention.

"Hello, earth to Mitch." She knocked on his head.

"Huh? Oh, sorry. Hi, Beth." He treated her to a dazzling smile, causing Raleigh to wonder if there wasn't a small spark of something between them. Beth would have told her if there was a bona fide romance, but she might keep it to herself if she only flirted a little. Or, she might be oblivious if Mitch was the one with a crush.

"Mitch, Raleigh has need of your expertise." She glanced at her watch. "And I've got work to do. Let me know, Raleigh." She hustled away, her bright pink jacket flapping behind her.

"What can I help you with today, Ms. Shinn?" Mitch asked in his exaggerated Louisiana drawl. He'd been brought up in Cajun country without much money, but his computer skills had been a ticket out of the boonies for him. That was how he put it, anyway.

"This is a personal matter." Raleigh rolled up a chair from a neighboring desk. "So if you have urgent foundation business, my problem can take a backseat."

"I got nothing pressing. What is it, Raleigh? You seem worried."

Did everyone see it? First Beth, now Mitch. If she

wasn't careful, her little problem would interfere with her ability to do her job.

"Can you hack into a bank's computer system?" she asked point-blank.

Mitch leaned back in his chair. "Well, now, that depends on which bank, and what information is needed. In general, the answer is no. Financial institution computer systems are pretty much hack-proof. But even if I could, I wouldn't. Not unless I want to spend ten-to-twenty in Huntsville."

"Ah." Briefly, she explained the problem. "Could it be a computer glitch?"

"Not likely. Probably the depositor did, in fact, type or write in your name and account number. Bank systems double-check such things to see that they match."

That was what she was afraid of. "Okay, then, what can you tell me about Griffin Benedict? I need to get this guy off my case."

Mitch grinned. "Now, that I can help with. But honestly, who would believe that you're engaged in criminal behavior? You're as straight as they come. I bet if I checked, I would find you've never even had a parking ticket. Hell, you probably are never late returning a library book."

He was absolutely right. Raleigh had high respect for the law. Her classmates in school had called her a Goody Two-shoes, but she couldn't help it. She liked rules. They made her comfortable. She'd been a rule-follower all her life.

"That's what makes this story so irresistible," she said, suddenly realizing the obvious. "Some sleaze-bag takes a bribe, no biggie. But an upright lawyer crusades for justice, then does something wildly immoral and illegal—that makes for good copy. Like a televangelist getting caught with a hooker."

Mitch looked thoughtful. "Griffin Benedict isn't known for taking cheap shots. His stories are well researched and are usually newsworthy. Picking on you seems a tad sensational for his style."

"You sound as if you like him."

"I never met him, but I read his stories."

"So, has he ever been sued for libel, or invasion of privacy? Does he cheat on his wife or his income taxes? Does he pad his expense report? I need something I can use to at least level the playing field."

"I'll try to have something for you by tomorrow."

GRIFFIN EYED the caller ID on his desk phone at work and lunged for the receiver, his heart pounding. This could be it.

"Griffin Benedict."

"Griffin, this is Pierce Fontaine at CNI. How are you today?"

Would the man sound so cheerful if he was about to deliver bad news? "I'm great, how about yourself?"

Griffin wanted to bite his tongue. He'd sounded too folksy, too…Southern. He had to garner a wide appeal if he wanted to succeed as a national TV journalist on *Currents,* the most watched news magazine on the planet.

"I wanted to let you know that we haven't yet reached a hiring decision," Pierce said. "I know you've been waiting a long time, but the brass—you know what sticklers upper management can be about these things."

"Is something in particular stopping them from giving the green light?" Griffin asked. If he knew what the problem was, maybe he could fix it.

"Well, the most obvious tick in the minus column is your lack of TV experience. Granted, you did amazingly well when we put you on camera, and test audiences love you. But you weren't under real-time deadline pressures."

Griffin knew that wouldn't be a problem. He thrived on deadlines. But the network wouldn't simply take his word. They would want proof.

"Then there's your…how do I say this? The bach-elor thing."

Griffin half laughed, half groaned. "I had nothing to do with that article. Came as a complete shock to me."

"Still, you do have a certain reputation with the ladies. *Currents* is a show that deals with serious issues. It's important we avoid any hint of scandal."

"I can assure you, my private life won't interfere with my work." He hadn't imagined his appeal with women would be a negative, but there wasn't much he could do about it so he quickly changed the subject. "Are there…other candidates vying for this position?" Of course there were. He wanted to know his competition.

"Actually, we have only one other candidate. He's also from your area—the brass think a Texan would round out the *Currents* team nicely. Paul Stratton, from KBBK. Know him?"

Griffin winced. Yeah, he knew Stratton. The guy was a pompous ass. Unfortunately, he also anchored the top-rated newscast in the whole South Texas market. He was good—had an enviable record as a journalist and even a Pulitzer under his belt. He had a few years on Griffin, and the TV creds Griffin lacked.

"Yeah, I know him," Griffin said, opting for the high road. "He'd be a good choice." If they could fit his ego through the newsroom door. Then he added, "I'd be better."

Pierce laughed, thankfully. "It's going to be a tough decision."

"Hey, what if I did some freelance stories for you?" It was a long shot; *Currents* used very few freelancers. "Roving reporter–type stuff, just me with a camera?"

Pierce didn't answer right away. Griffin crossed his fingers.

Finally the CNI news director responded. "Did you have any particular stories in mind?"

Griffin's heart pounded. Did he dare mention it? He hadn't yet told his editor about the Raleigh Shinn story. Griffin might get himself fired if he offered it to someone else. He decided to take the chance.

"I'm working on something…it's connected to Project Justice—are you familiar with them?"

"Yes, indeed." Griffin could almost hear the man salivating.

"I've uncovered a possible breach of ethics there. Nothing that's ready to air," he added hastily.

"When do you think you'll have something?"

Griffin pulled a number out of thin air. "A couple of weeks." Surely by then he would have enough information to nail Raleigh Shinn to the wall.

"I'll tell the brass to count on it."

## CHAPTER THREE

As RALEIGH EXITED the courthouse the following day, the hairs on the back of her neck stood at attention. Someone was definitely watching her.

Earlier that day, she had dismissed the tickle at her nape as paranoia, a result of nerves or not enough sleep. But her instincts rarely failed her, and they certainly wouldn't do so repeatedly. There couldn't be any doubt she was being followed.

Since it was such a beautiful fall day, and since she had been neglecting her workouts lately, she had decided to walk from the Project Justice office to the courthouse, where she had filed a motion to overturn Lewis Rhiner's conviction based on the new DNA evidence.

That taken care of, she'd planned a quick lunch at a nearby bagel shop, after which she would pay a visit to the police department and personally make sure they were following up on the new suspect.

But first she had to figure out who was watching her. Not that she didn't have a pretty good idea.

She walked briskly down the street, turned a

corner, then ducked into a doorway like she'd seen people do in the movies. Then she waited.

About thirty seconds later, a black Mustang came around the corner and pulled into a parking space across the street from her vantage place. But the driver—anonymous behind tinted windows—didn't turn off the engine or get out right away.

Bingo.

She'd noticed this same car earlier. Normally she wouldn't have taken note, but it was almost the exact car Jason used to drive, just a slightly newer model. The Mustang had been parked on the street near her apartment building when she had exited that morning, and for one brief, insane moment, she had expected to see Jason climb out from behind the wheel.

Then she'd remembered that Jason was dead. Silly how one sensory trigger—a car, a song, a certain wine—could bring it all back.

Raleigh was pretty sure the Mustang's driver couldn't see her. She stood in the shadow of the doorway, peeking out every few seconds.

After about a minute, the driver killed the engine and opened the door. Though she couldn't see the man's face, she recognized his body immediately— the white T-shirt stretched across broad shoulders, tapering down to a narrow waist, the worn denim riding low on his lean hips, and that butt—definitely drool-worthy, to use Beth's terminology.

Raleigh's face heated. She was mortified by her

reaction to Griffin Benedict. The man was trying to ruin her, and all she could do about it was notice how sexy he was?

Griffin peered up and down the street, shading his face with his hand against the noonday sun. Raleigh shrank back into the shadows. After a few moments she dared another peek. He was heading her way.

She intended to confront him, but on her terms. So she entered the store in whose doorway she had been lurking. It was a small drugstore, more of a snack shop, really. She ducked behind a rack of chips, peeking between the bags of Fritos and SunChips.

Griffin entered and scanned the store. *Oh, God, don't let him find me like this, hiding behind junk food!* As he ventured farther into the store, she ducked into a different aisle.

After a few moments, apparently satisfied she wasn't in the store, he left.

She hurried after him. *I've got you now.*

The next door down was a hair salon. Griffin entered. Raleigh quickened her pace to catch up, then stood just outside the door, flattened against the wall. She felt ridiculous, and silently cursed him for forcing her to resort to this childish behavior.

He exited only a few seconds later and she popped away from the wall, nearly colliding with him.

"Hello, Mr. Benedict."

"Holy shit!"

She enjoyed the surprised look on his face. Probably few people ever got the jump on this guy.

"I'm tired of you following me," she said. "I want you to stop."

"I wasn't—"

"Don't waste your breath. I saw you outside my apartment this morning. You must be getting some riveting footage." She nodded at the tiny video camera dangling around his neck. "Just what, exactly, are you hoping I'll do? Incriminate myself? You'll wait a long time for that."

For a long moment, Griffin just stared at her as if appraising his chances of lying his way out of this. No way. She'd caught him fair and square.

He stared for so long, she had to resist the urge to squirm and look away. What did he see? She had an insane suspicion he could read her mind. No: if that were the case, he would see she was innocent of any wrongdoing.

And he would see her other thoughts, those inappropriate ones involving naked flesh, entwined limbs and tangled sheets. Oh, Lord, she had to stop thinking of him that way.

His sexy mouth pursed, and she thought he might be trying not to laugh. Damn it, she was not supposed to be amusing. She had worked long and hard to come off as intimidating.

Clearly he wasn't intimidated.

"All right, yes, I was following you. I was hoping you might do something…interesting."

"Like what? Strip naked on Main Street?"

"Now, that *would* make for interesting footage."

She gasped in a breath. His attitude wasn't helping matters. The unholy light behind those sincere brown eyes hinted that his thoughts were as impure as hers.

"Wait a minute. You're a newspaper reporter. Why do you want video footage?"

He cocked his head but didn't answer.

"Are you going to keep following me?"

Griffin shrugged one careless shoulder. "Wouldn't be much point, now that you're onto me."

"Good thing, because stalking is against the law. I could have you arrested."

"Nice try, but you'd be a little short on evidence."

Her blood heated up a notch, and not just from overactive hormones. She was really mad, and the fact that he was so calm, so…amused, just made her want to spit in his eye.

*Don't let it show. Don't let it show.*

"Our business is concluded, then, wouldn't you say?" Maybe this would be the end of it. She tried to step around him, but he blocked her path.

"Just a minute. I have more questions for you." He had the nerve to lift the video camera, point it at her and turn it on. A blinking red light told her she was on camera.

She definitely knew better than to lose her composure when a camera was rolling. "Ask away. What would you like to know, Mr. Benedict?"

"I thought we were on a first-name basis."

"Did you have a question for me?"

"Yes. In the past month, how many times would you say you've spoken to Leo Simonetti?"

The question caught her off guard. "You mean Anthony. Anthony Simonetti is my client."

"No, I meant Leo. Anthony's father."

Raleigh quickly regained her composure. "In that case, the answer is zero. I have no dealings with Leo Simonetti. The only other member of Anthony's family I'm in contact with is Connie, his sister."

"Really."

"Yes, really. What's your point here?"

Still filming, Griffin pulled a creased piece of paper from the back pocket of his jeans. Another photocopy? What now? He handed the paper to Raleigh, and she unfolded it. It was a copy of her cell phone bill. One phone number, which appeared numerous times, was highlighted in yellow.

Raleigh didn't immediately recognize the number, but that didn't mean much. She made hundreds of phone calls in a month.

"Do you recognize that piece of paper?" Griffin asked.

"It appears to be a copy of my cell phone bill, although I cannot, at this time, confirm the information it contains as genuine. Again, obtained illegally, as no one but me should have access."

He brushed aside the question of legality as easily as he would a mosquito. "Do you know whose number that is, highlighted in yellow?"

"No, I don't. Enlighten me." If Griffin thought it belonged to Leo Simonetti, he was crazy. But whoever it was, she'd called him or her a lot. She examined the paper more closely. She'd called this person at all hours, too—daytime, evening, weekends, and… at 2:30 a.m.? She never called anyone at that hour. She would have been asleep.

Had anyone else had access to her phone late at night? No, absolutely not.

Griffin Benedict's next words were spoken with relish. "The number belongs to Leo Simonetti,"

Criminy. She couldn't panic. Not when the camera was rolling. "Turn the camera off, please."

"Why? Did I hit a nerve?"

She folded her arms and waited. She wouldn't say another word until he complied with her request, but she wouldn't run away, either. She would stand here and smile at the dead air he was collecting on his camera.

Finally, with a sigh, he lowered the camera. The red light went off. "Do you have something to say?"

"I don't know who the number belongs to," she began. "But I have never spoken with Leo Simonetti

in my life. Not once." She took out her BlackBerry.
"If I ever called that number, it will be in my call
history." She scrolled through her list of outgoing
calls. It went back as far as a week. No sign of the
mystery telephone number.

She handed the phone to Griffin. "Check for
yourself."

He did. He scrolled through the list, then checked
the phone bill again. "This phone bill covers a time
period before last week."

She pinched the bridge of her nose, then snatched
her phone back. "Has it ever occurred to you that
your source, whoever it might be, is playing you?
That someone is trying to embarrass me, publicly,
or worse, and they're using you to do it?"

He handed the phone back to her. "I don't think
that's the case."

"So, who's your source? I have a right to know
who is saying these terrible, false things about me."

He flashed a disarming smile. "Now, you know a
good journalist doesn't reveal his sources."

"Who says you're a good journalist?" It was a low
blow, and though she was fed up with Griffin Benedict and his lying source, she immediately regretted
her words. Griffin Benedict might be tenacious, and
he might be distractingly sexy, but he appeared to be
a good journalist.

So far.

"I guess you're not a fan," he said, not seeming troubled by the fact.

"The funny thing is, I am. I mean, I've read a few of your articles. Although the stories you pursue are…out there, and your writing style is…irreverent, you don't strike me as careless or foolhardy. You don't pander. I would go so far as to say you don't even go for sensationalism.

"So why this story? It doesn't seem your style."

"Anything that involves human emotions, human weaknesses, is my style. I've found that subjects intriguing to me also draw in my readers. For whatever reason, I find you and your possible ethics violation highly intriguing."

"Well, your publisher isn't going to be so intrigued when the *Telegram* gets slapped with a libel suit. And don't start with your 'public figure' nonsense." Public figures had to prove malice in order to win a libel claim—a pretty high standard. "I'm not a public figure. I'm simply doing my job. I have never sought fame or publicity."

"Even if you were a public figure, I wouldn't print anything that wasn't a provable truth. You have my word on that."

His word. As if that counted for anything. She didn't even know the man. Yet, for some reason, his promise did reassure her slightly.

Oh, man, where was she going with this? Could

a handsome face and a charming smile disarm her to
the point she could no longer use her brain?

"I'm happy to hear you won't print lies about me.
Now, then, about this phone bill. I have a theory."

"Let's hear it."

"If that's Leo Simonetti's number, then this isn't
really my bill. Someone got a copy of my bill and
doctored it, adding in this suspicious phone number.
It's incredibly easy to do. We have a guy on our
staff, Mitch Delacroix, who specializes in all kinds
of computer and document fraud. You wouldn't believe the stuff that can be done with a good graphics
program."

"Nice try."

"I'm serious. And if I'm right, I can prove it. I just
paid this phone bill. I have it filed away. We can go
to my apartment, and I'll show it to you."

Benedict's eyes lit up. "That's an excellent idea.
I'll drive."

Griffin could hardly believe his good luck. Raleigh
Shinn had just invited him to see inside her home.
He could learn all kinds of things about a person by
seeing what they surrounded themselves with, what
was important to them. Family pictures displayed
on the mantel, mail left carelessly on a table, trash
in a wastebasket all could speak volumes. Even a
subject's housekeeping habits were revealing about
character.

But his excitement over Raleigh's invitation was

tinged with unease. What if she was right? Obviously his anonymous source had an ax to grind with either Raleigh or Project Justice. But what if the ammunition they were using was bogus? Manufactured? And he'd fallen for it?

Not only had he fallen for it, he'd bet his career on it. If he called Pierce Fontaine and told him the story was a nonstarter, he could kiss the anchor job goodbye.

He tried not to think about that. Surely Raleigh hadn't expected him to call her bluff, go to her apartment and look at her phone bills. Surely at the last minute, she wouldn't be able to locate the pertinent bill.

"Turn right at the light," Raleigh said. She had spoken a bare minimum to him since they'd climbed into his Mustang. Smart lady. Most people, when being nailed to the wall by a reporter, tended to talk too much, digging their graves deeper and deeper.

This subject, at least, knew when to keep her mouth shut.

Or maybe she simply couldn't stand him and didn't want to talk to him.

He didn't like that idea. Yeah, his reporting made plenty of people mad. But a woman, he could usually charm. Women liked him, even when he was putting them through the wringer. A smile, a wink, a touch of sincere interest, and they spilled their guts. Some of them seemed relieved to release their burden of secrets. He had learned more dirt by spending time with some guy's wife or girlfriend than by any other method.

His charms didn't seem to work on Raleigh. He couldn't deny he felt something there, some spark of sexual recognition. The fact she was such a hard nut to crack made her even more appealing. But she wasn't going to slip up and admit anything. She was too skillful with her words for that. He bet she had seen all the ways a criminal can mess up, and learned from their mistakes.

Raleigh finally broke the silence. "Next block. The tall white building with the—oh, wait, you already know where I live. Hard to find street parking this time of day."

"I'm lucky when it comes to parking."

If he was really lucky, he would leave her building with something he could run with. She had no idea how dangerous he could be, let loose in her home. And if he was *really* lucky, they would take a looooong lunch…

Hell, he had no business thinking like that. The CNI people were watching his every move. A sexual liaison with the subject of his story, or even a background source, would be just the sort of thing they didn't want to see.

Still, his fantasies persisted. He would take off those glasses, unbutton the suit jacket, which was far too warm for this mild day. He would slide his hands inside that silky blouse—

"You just missed a parking space." Raleigh sounded exasperated.

Griffin slammed on his brakes. He waited until traffic cleared and put the car in Reverse.

"You're going to get a ticket, driving like that on a busy downtown street."

"It wouldn't be the first time." He got lots of tickets. The Houston police knew his car on sight. Fortunately, he had a lady friend who was a judge. Even though they were no longer involved, she usually made his tickets disappear.

"So, how do you like living downtown?" he asked, just trying to get the conversational ball rolling. He wouldn't have pegged her as a downtowner. She seemed more the type to live in a cushy condo in Memorial or the Galleria area. "What made you move here?"

"The path of least resistance," she said, more under her breath than to him. She got out and, quarters already in her hand, started pumping them into the meter.

"I can do that."

"My idea to come here, I'll pay the parking fee," she said. "Besides, I wouldn't want you to write that I'd accepted payment from you."

Touché.

"What do you mean, the path of least resistance?"

he asked as they climbed the stairs to the ornate, brass front door.

"I needed a place to live. I found this one at a good price, close to work, so I took it. No big mystery."

But it was. He sensed she wasn't telling him the whole story.

The lobby of her building was 1920s Art Deco splendor, with vaulted ceilings, square columns, potted palm trees and brass accents. The old-fashioned elevator was trimmed in brass, with one of those inner metal doors that had to be closed manually.

Inside the elevator, Raleigh stood as close to the wall as she could—as far away from him as possible—and looked anywhere but at him.

This was no good. He wanted her to be comfortable with him. When people got comfortable they let down their guard. Did this woman ever let down her guard?

They got out on the third floor. Raleigh extracted her key chain from her purse. The key chain was a basic, utilitarian ring with a small LED flashlight attached. It told him nothing about her except that she was practical. No tiny frames with pictures of children or a boyfriend, no souvenir trinkets from vacations, not even a symbol of her work.

He fully expected her apartment to be the same— dull, functional. So when she opened the front door and admitted him, he had a shock.

Clean, neat, organized—it was all those things. No surprises there. But it was colorful. Her walls were painted in vibrant shades of turquoise, moss green, rich gold. The hardwood floors were covered with good wool rugs in contemporary geometric patterns—no fusty Oriental rugs passed down from family. The sofa and two matching chairs were upholstered in cream-colored silk, with throw pillows in every shade of the rainbow.

She had art on the walls—real art, not just some boring framed picture of a mountain to fill a spot. The abstract paintings screamed emotion.

The room was such a contrast to the woman he had so far seen that he was confused.

"Do you live here alone?" Maybe a roommate was responsible for the decor.

Before she could answer, a rust-colored ball of fur streaked into the room, barking wildly.

"Copper! That's enough," Raleigh scolded. But she leaned down and scooped the tiny dog—a Pomeranian, Griffin thought—into her arms and let it lick her face. "Yes, baby, I'm home at a strange hour. I surprised you, didn't I?" Her sweet, maternal-sounding voice was totally different than the voice she used with humans.

Finally she turned back to Griffin, looking slightly embarrassed. "Yes, I live alone except for this little guy. Why?"

He shrugged. "No reason." *Except that you have*

*a split personality.* "I never expected you to have an ankle-biter yappy dog."

Raleigh set the dog down on the rug with a quick scratch behind the ears. "He's an excellent watchdog. A woman living alone needs some protection."

Griffin tried not to laugh. "Oh, yeah, he's a big threat." He stooped down and held his hand out. The dog eyed him warily. "I won't hurt you, little guy."

"If you'll wait here, please, I'll go get the phone bill. I know right where it is."

As soon as she left the room, the dog ventured closer, sniffing the air. But when Griffin tried to pet him, he skittered away. That was when Griffin noticed an antique walnut table in a far corner of the living room that was covered with framed pictures and all manner of knickknacks—a potential gold mine of data.

Forget the dog—although the fact she had a pet was an interesting tidbit.

On closer inspection, he realized every one of the half-dozen or so pictures on the table was of a man—the same man. Some were formal portraits at different ages, others casual snapshots. In some, he was with a beautiful woman.

With a start, he recognized the woman as Raleigh. She wore her hair in a completely different style— loose and wavy. In one picture, it fell in loose auburn curls well past her shoulders. She didn't wear glasses, clunky or otherwise, in any of the pictures. And her figure?

Yowza. Just as he'd suspected, she *was* a hot babe.

He quickly came back to earth, however. The man, obviously, was her dead husband, and this table was a shrine to his memory. There were framed ticket stubs to a Broadway show, dried flowers, a smooth stone probably plucked from a river or beach. A poem written in a girlish hand.

A widow was allowed to honor her husband, he supposed, but this was way, way over the top. It had been more than six years. Was she still that hung up on the guy?

It was hard to know what she must feel. He had never lost anyone that close. Maybe he'd never *had* anyone that close. He felt a pang of sympathy for the pain she must carry with her every day, though she didn't let it show. He also felt a thread of regret for something in his own life that could never, ever be.

Not that he stood much chance of getting past the woman's facade, given that his goal was to seriously tarnish her reputation and possibly cost her her job. But now, he didn't even feel comfortable fantasizing. Her handsome husband, who would forever be young and smiling in her mind, would always stand squarely between them.

"I can't find the damn bill," Raleigh announced as she reentered the living room. "I tried going online, but my password isn't working—" She came to a halt when she spotted him standing before Jason's shrine.

"I'm sorry, I didn't mean to snoop," he said, actually meaning it.

"If I didn't want people to see Jason's pictures, I wouldn't put them in the living room." The frost was back in her voice.

Yeah, but how many people did she actually invite into her home? Not many, he guessed.

Griffin felt he ought to say *something*. "It must have been awful. You obviously loved him very much."

Raleigh blinked several times. "I did… I still do. He was the—" Suddenly she hardened. "Oh, no you don't."

"I'm sorry?" What had he done now?

"You aren't going to weasel personal information out of me using the sympathy card, just so you can exploit me in your damn newspaper."

"I wouldn't," he said. He never claimed to be a paragon of virtue, but he wouldn't stoop to exploit a woman's grief for her husband. Her former marriage had nothing to do with the story.

"Convenient, you losing the bill."

"I pay it online. It's possible I didn't get a paper one, and didn't notice. Someone could have stolen it from my mailbox. The lock isn't all that secure."

"Mmm-hmm." He congratulated himself for

predicting the outcome of this meeting so accurately. Was he a good judge of character, or what?

"Of course you don't believe me." She shook her head. "I guess I can't blame you for your suspicions. It looks bad. The phony bill, the deposit…"

"Yes, what about that deposit?"

"I don't know where that deposit came from!" she said hotly. "It simply appeared. I called the bank, and they say it wasn't an error. I can put you in touch with any number of bank personnel I spoke with, right on up to a vice president. Some of them, I spoke with long before my first meeting with you. The day after the deposit was made, in fact, I was on the phone, trying to figure out where that money belonged, because I knew it wasn't mine. I took detailed notes during the conversation."

He pulled out his notebook. "Okay, let's have the names."

"Mr. Temple. He's a vice president. He's the one I spoke with most recently. The others are written down at work. I'll e-mail them to you."

"Okay. We'll do this the slow and painful way. Sure you don't want to just tell me the truth now?"

"I can't confess to something I didn't do. Don't you see? Someone is trying to ruin my reputation. And they're using you to do the job."

That statement made him pause. What if she was right? What if someone had made Raleigh Shinn the target of a smear campaign based on lies, making

Griffin a patsy? If he went public with something he hadn't independently verified—and thank God he wasn't that stupid—he would be in the unemployment line and possibly the defendant in a libel lawsuit.

Part of him wanted to turn loose of Raleigh. She seemed genuine. But if he let go of this story now, after he'd promised it to CNI, he wouldn't have a shot at the anchor job.

Unless…unless he figured a way to turn the story to his benefit.

Maybe, if Raleigh *thought* he was on her side, she would let down her guard. "I'll talk to the bank employees," he said, trying to inject some sympathy into his voice. "If someone is trying to ruin you, we have to stop them."

"We?" She looked at him as if he was crazy. "There's no 'we' here. I believe our business has concluded for now."

"Raleigh, maybe you don't realize the seriousness of what's going on here. You could be in danger."

"Please."

Griffin sat up straighter. If she was telling the truth, this could be an even better story than he first thought. Someone was going to a great deal of trouble to ruin Raleigh Shinn and, by inference, the whole of Project Justice. Why?

He took out his notebook. "Who are your enemies? Whose bad side have you gotten on lately? Who might want to hurt you?"

"Oh, no. You're not turning this into another story."

"We could help each other," he pointed out. "You scratch my back, I'll scratch yours. I can figure out who's doing this and stop them before he or she does permanent harm to your career."

"I don't partner with journalists."

"You don't understand. I'm being considered for a national TV job. A hot story like this would help me land it. And I could give Project Justice some positive press."

"Talk to our public relations coordinator, then."

But he could see the indecision playing on her face. She knew he could slice and dice her in the press, or make her look like Joan of Arc.

"If you're really innocent of any wrongdoing, your cooperation could—"

"No," she said suddenly. "I want you to leave. We're done."

That's where Raleigh was wrong. She didn't know it yet, but things between them were just getting started.

# CHAPTER FOUR

BETH STUCK her head into Raleigh's office. "You up for lunch?"

Raleigh was tempted. But she looked at the huge stack of paper on her desk that was the transcript from the original Simonetti trial, and shook her head. She'd been reading the transcript for hours, and had many hours to go. The original trial had lasted a ridiculous six weeks.

"I can't. Too much work."

Beth stepped inside. "Daniel wouldn't approve. You know how important it is to rest and refuel."

Raleigh pulled off her glasses and rubbed her eyes. Beth was right. But work seemed to be the only way she could keep Griffin Benedict off her mind. It was like the guy had planted a seed in her brain, where it had firmly taken root.

*You scratch my back, I'll scratch yours.*

She had emailed him all the names of the people she'd talked to at her bank, and she had given the bank permission to discuss the matter of the mystery deposit with Griffin. And she'd finally gotten into her cell phone provider's website and emailed a copy of the phone bill in question. She assumed she wouldn't hear from him again, a thought that should have pleased her.

"Maybe lunch is a good idea." Beth would no doubt have some distracting story to tell during lunch. She was one of those people to whom strange things always happened.

"Did someone say lunch?" Mitch Delacroix slipped through the open office door behind Beth.

Great. Now Raleigh's office was Grand Central Station.

"I'm trying to drag Raleigh's nose away from the grindstone," Beth said. "Want to come with us?"

Mitch looked undecided then abruptly shook his head. "Can't. Meeting. I just stopped by to give you this, Raleigh." He held out a bulging manila folder.

Raleigh couldn't remember asking Mitch for research with any of her cases. She must have looked at him blankly.

"Griffin Benedict?"

"Ohhh." She slapped a hand to her forehead. "Mitch, I'm so sorry to have put you to a lot of trouble for nothing. I don't believe Griffin Benedict will bother me again."

Mitch shrugged. "It's okay. Digging up dirt on people is fun for me, you know that, and I didn't have anything else urgent—or half as interesting. Glad you worked it out, though."

He handed Raleigh the folder. "Enjoy it. Then

shred the contents, okay? A few bits and pieces in there aren't, ah, fully in the public domain."

Meaning he'd done some hacking. On her behalf. Raleigh felt guilty as hell.

She set the folder on her desk, grabbed her purse and headed for the door. "Does Lancer Steak-house sound okay to you? They have good lunch specials."

"Wait!" Beth's single word stuck her to the floor.

"What?"

"Aren't you going to look inside the folder?"

"No way," Raleigh said. "I no longer need information on the man. It wouldn't be ethical for me to snoop—"

"Ethical, shmethical. This will make excellent lunch entertainment." Beth grabbed the folder. "Let's go."

"I don't think we should read the information on Griffin," Raleigh said again a couple of minutes later as she signed out. Celeste seemed to be heavily involved in a Danielle Steele novel.

"But aren't you curious?"

"Curiosity killed the cat."

Celeste gave a disapproving harrumph, reminding Raleigh that even when she seemed not to be paying attention, she was. Celeste was a little sharper than most people gave her credit for.

"Look, Beth," Raleigh said once they'd exited the building into a gloomy, overcast day. "I think I've convinced Griffin of my innocence. He's not going to print any lies about me. End of threat, as far as I'm concerned."

"But you don't know what he's really planning to write. Even if he told you he believed you—reporters can say anything. You should be ready. Just in case. Knowledge is power."

"And you're grasping at straws because you're nosy. I had a hard enough time ejecting him from my apartment yesterday—"

Beth gasped. "He was in your apartment?"

Raleigh's face warmed as she imagined what Beth was thinking. "I brought him there to show him evidence that would exonerate me. He seemed convinced. He even warned me that I might be in danger."

Again, Beth gasped. "Maybe you are!"

Raleigh waved away her concern. "People who commit crimes with paper and computers seldom turned to guns, knives or bombs. He was just trying to manipulate my feelings, so I would agree to…" Agree to what? She wasn't sure.

"Anyway," she concluded, "I'm done with him."

"Well," said Beth, "if you won't look at the folder, that's your business. But I'm going to check it out."

Raleigh knew she wouldn't dissuade her friend, so she didn't argue further. In truth, she was curious about the contents of that folder.

Getting Griffin to leave her apartment hadn't been

easy, but evicting him from her mind was proving impossible. She kept seeing him as he'd looked, large and masculine and utterly out of place in her feminine living room. Her stomach swooped every time that image jumped into her consciousness.

His presence had felt exciting and dangerous, representing everything she tried to avoid in her life. Part of her had wanted to grab a broom and sweep him out into the hallway; another part had almost invited him to have dinner with her. She loved to cook, yet how long had it been since she'd done more than toss a frozen dinner into the microwave?

She and Beth headed for Lancer and got a booth in the back with a bit of privacy. After ordering, Beth opened the folder with obvious anticipation and began sifting through the contents, scanning pages that interested her.

"Seems the journalist has been the subject of more than a few interviews," she said.

Raleigh put her fingers in her ears. "La la la, I'm not listening." But of course, she was.

"Born and raised in Houston," Beth said as she scanned one of the articles, which looked to have been copied from the internet. "Humble beginnings, broken home, rags to riches…wow, he really overcame some tough odds to get where he is."

"If that's even true. He could have made it all up. Not all reporters check their facts."

"He went to University of Texas on a scholarship.

Good for him. Oh, look, his college transcript. Almost straight A's."

That was a little surprising. Raleigh would have pegged him as the kind who partied his way through college.

"Graduate school, University of Oklahoma," Beth continued. "I wouldn't have guessed he was the academic type."

"I wouldn't, either." Raleigh was getting sucked in, despite herself.

"He's not all about books and classrooms, though. He has a black belt in judo."

"Now that doesn't surprise me." The way he moved, so decisively but at the same time with grace, suggested some type of athletic training.

"Seems he paid his dues, working at small papers, stringing for the wire services, freelancing for magazines, including—" Beth smiled "—*Soldier of Fortune.*"

"A magazine for mercenaries and assorted gun nuts. Nice."

"Then the *Telegram* hired him. That's when he started to make a name for himself—oh, look at this. A copy of his driver's license. He lives on The Heights Boulevard. Cool neighborhood."

His address put him squarely inside the Loop. The Heights was an up-and-coming area with plenty of young professionals and lots of parks for them to play in on the weekends.

"Here's the 'Most Eligible Bachelors' story. Want to read it? That's totally available to anyone, no invasion of privacy."

"I'm not interested," Raleigh said flatly as she copped a peek at the color printout of the story, which featured a large picture of Griffin leaning against a brick wall, looking tough and slightly cynical—and heart-stoppingly gorgeous.

Beth sifted through a few more photos. "Seems he was into the club scene for a bit—pretty models hanging on him. He doesn't look particularly happy."

Which gave Raleigh a perverse sense of satisfaction. From her ivory tower, she liked to think that no one in the club scene was happy, filling their empty lives with drinking and drugs and meaningless banter.

"Poor guy," she said. "Rough life having to hang with gorgeous women."

"The boy likes to drive fast. Look at all these speeding tickets. His car insurance rates must be through the roof."

"Beth, enough."

"Wait—oh, hmm. Interesting."

The waitress chose that moment to bring their salads and baked potatoes. Beth closed the folder and suddenly seemed keen on loading her spud with butter, sour cream and bacon.

Raleigh added a few drops of dressing to her salad and a sprinkle of pepper to her potato. They ate for a few minutes in silence before Raleigh couldn't stand it anymore.

"What's so interesting?"

"Hmm?"

"You saw something in that folder and you said, 'Hmmm. Interesting.'"

"Did I?" Beth pretended to look confused. "I thought you didn't want to know."

"Okay, I'm a big liar. I'm fascinated. There, satisfied?"

Beth grinned and opened the folder back up. "He was nominated for a Pulitzer. Did a piece on war orphans in Afghanistan."

"I remember that story," Raleigh said suddenly. "It ran in the *Telegram*'s Sunday magazine, couple of years ago." She apparently hadn't paid much attention to who had written the piece, but now the details poured back into her mind. It was one of the most compassionate, emotional pieces of writing she'd ever read. Griffin hadn't just reported a sad situation, he had immersed himself in it. Those children and their tragedy weren't simply statistics to him. They were real people he'd taken the time to know.

The story had made her cry.

It was hard to dislike, or even dismiss, a man like that.

RALEIGH TOLD HERSELF a million times that it didn't make any difference whether he truly cared about his subjects or was an opportunistic paparazzo. He was not her concern anymore.

When she returned to the office, she had an email from Daniel advising her that Channel 6 had aired a small story during their Noon News about the handgun found in the water heater. Amazing how he always seemed to know when anything involving Project Justice aired or was printed or tweeted.

With a knot in her stomach, Raleigh watched the video clip attached to Daniel's email. A female reporter with a heavy drawl interviewed the property owner who had found the gun when he'd replaced his water heater.

"I wasn't living here at the time," the neighbor said. "But it freaks me out that a murder weapon was right here under my nose."

"Alleged murder weapon," Raleigh murmured.

The report showed some photos of the rusty-looking gun, then focused on the homeowner's overblown emotions concerning the discovery.

At the very end of the piece, the reporter said only that the gun was too corroded for identification.

Huh. Second reporter to bring up the corrosion. Someone from the police department was feeding information to the press. It somehow made her feel better that Griffin wasn't the only one who knew things. He didn't have magical powers, he merely knew a blabbermouth cop.

But the media was wrong about one thing. Although

the gun was corroded, it wasn't beyond hope. Praktech Laboratories, a highly regarded independent lab that did specialized evidence analysis, was working on the weapon.

No one from the station had contacted her for information. In fact, Project Justice hadn't been mentioned. Maybe that was a good thing. It was hard for her and the other investigators to do their jobs in a fishbowl.

Though she loved her work, Raleigh was glad when her workday was over and she could head home. She parked her Volvo in the garage beneath her building, then unlocked the steel security door and climbed the stairs to her third-floor apartment. Her heart lifted as she entered her beautiful oasis and saw Copper bouncing around on his hind legs, wanting to be held.

Raleigh picked up the little dog and pressed her face against the soft fur. Nothing relieved stress like a warm, furry little dog. She hugged him until he squirmed to get down.

"Did ya miss me, boy?" she asked.

Jason had given Copper to Raleigh as a gift not long before he died. They used to bring him to the office, where someone was usually around to take him out for walks and keep him company. Bringing him to work at Project Justice wasn't practical, though. Now, a neighbor walked him at midday, but he spent quite a few hours alone.

Copper had been a great comfort to her in the days after Jason's death, the one constant in a world gone topsy-turvy. She wouldn't know what to do without him.

She quickly changed into a Houston Astros T-shirt, a pair of sweats and walking shoes. This was her favorite time of day, taking Copper for his walk, when she could clear her mind and stretch her muscles. Her building had a gym she could use anytime, but she preferred a peaceful walk.

Raleigh grabbed her cell phone from her purse and stuck it in her pocket, then clipped Copper's leash to his collar and took him downstairs via the elevator—the stairs were a bit much for his tiny legs.

Irving, the doorman, greeted her with a nod and opened the door for her. His presence was Daniel's doing. Usually only the most posh apartment buildings enjoyed such a luxury, but Daniel was serious about his employees' safety, and a number of them lived at this address.

Soon she and Copper were on their way along their usual route, surrounded by commuters and pedestrians heading home, but still alone.

Her thoughts turned to Griffin, and that war-orphan story he'd written. She couldn't figure out who he really was—bottom-feeder reporter, out to nail a sensational story no matter who he had to stomp on, or a compassionate journalist, shining a light in dark corners, revealing truths? It bugged her that she couldn't peg him. She was normally pretty good at peeling away fake facades and ulterior motives, but she didn't feel she'd figured out the real Griffin Benedict.

She was only a couple of blocks from home when her cell rang. This time, it played the theme song to the *Perry Mason* show.

"Very funny, guys." Someone at the office was always downloading ridiculous ringtones onto her phone. She still had no idea who the culprit was.

She stopped to let Copper sniff at a particularly intriguing bush as she dug the phone out of her pocket and glanced at the caller ID. Anonymous.

A lot of the people she talked to, like cops and other lawyers, were freakish about privacy. With a shrug, she answered. "Raleigh Shinn."

The weird, tinny voice that greeted her sent a shiver through her body. "Miss Shinn. It's not a good idea to continue your quest to free Anthony Simonetti."

"Who am I speaking with, please?" She ordered her voice to remain calm, though she felt an urge to fling her phone into a nearby bush as if it were a poisonous snake.

"Who I am is not important. You should know, though, that the man is guilty."

"Really? What makes you such an expert on the subject?"

"He told me he did it. He had no reason to lie. The right man is paying the price for that murder."

"Who are you? I can't take you seriously until I know who I'm dealing with."

"You'd better take me seriously. Or it's more than your reputation on the line."

"Are you threatening me?"

"I'm an Astros fan, too." The caller disconnected.

Raleigh suddenly felt as vulnerable as if she were walking naked down the street. The caller could see her. Right now.

She whirled around, checking out nearby cars and pedestrians. No one acted suspiciously. But all those buildings surrounding her, all those dark windows.

In a hurry to get somewhere safe, she picked up Copper and walked—quickly but not running—toward the front door of her building.

She'd almost made it to a safe haven when she heard footsteps behind her. Faster, closer.

"Raleigh, wait up."

She whirled around and nearly collided with Griffin. "What are you doing here?" she demanded.

"What happened? Who was on the phone?"

"How did you—"

"I was watching you, okay? You looked upset. No, you looked terrified."

"I have to get inside. Someone is watching me.

Someone besides you. He…he saw what I was wearing."

Griffin tensed and looked around, automatically moving to shield her from the street. "C'mon, let's go." He put an arm around her shoulders and escorted her the half block to her door. The doorman gave her a questioning look.

"It's okay, Irving, I know him." She didn't, not really. But his concern seemed genuine.

Once in the safety of her building's beautiful lobby, she took a few deep breaths.

"Tell me what happened," Griffin said gently.

She couldn't help herself—she spilled everything. "Anonymous caller. He was using something to change his voice, so he sounded like a robot, or a computer."

"Did he threaten you?"

"Not in so many words. But he was watching me. He knew what I was wearing. Oh, God, it was so creepy."

It had to be the same person who'd given Griffin the bogus information, and made the deposit. Which meant Griffin was right. Her enemy was upping the stakes. His veiled threat could mean anything, up to and including physical harm.

"You should call the police," Griffin said.

"Yes. Right." She still had her cell phone in her hand. Halfway through dialing 911, however, she stopped. "The police won't care. They have better things to do than track down crank callers."

She knew the drill. First of all, they couldn't get access to cell phone records without a court order. Even if she cleared that hurdle, tracking down the call wouldn't help. Her caller could have used a pay phone or a throwaway cell. Criminals were savvy these days. They watched crime shows like everyone else and knew how other criminals had been tripped up.

But the police wouldn't go to that much trouble, anyway. They would write it off as a joke or assume she was trying to generate publicity to support some crazy conspiracy theory regarding Anthony. She wasn't exactly tops on their list of lovable people right now, since proving Anthony's innocence would be a huge embarrassment to them.

She would tell Daniel about it. He had access to all kinds of security experts and bodyguards. He would know what measures were appropriate. Daniel didn't much care for law enforcement, as a rule, and could she blame him, after he'd spent six years on death row?

"Should I be worried that you're still watching me?" Raleigh asked. "You did receive the email I sent, right? With the *real* cell phone bill, and the names of the bank employees?"

If he heard her question, he was ignoring it. "I

knew there was a story here. I couldn't give up. And I was right. Someone is out to get you."

Raleigh's knees felt shaky. "I could use a glass of wine. How about you?" It was the least she could do after he'd come to her rescue. He'd seemed genuinely concerned.

Unless…he'd been the one to make the call? How stupid could she be that she hadn't considered that possibility before? Quite a coincidence, Griffin just happening to be Johnny-on-the-spot when she received a personal threat.

She should have told him to hit the road. But that seemed ungrateful.

Touching her wedding ring, she winced. *Sorry, Jason.* She was rattled, and not thinking or acting like her usual self. But she had to admit, as scared as she was about that phone call, she didn't mind having a strong, capable male in full protective mode watching out for her.

Raleigh wiped her damp palms on her sweatpants, wishing she was still wearing her suit, her armor against the world. The gray knit fabric molded to her body, revealing more than she was comfortable with.

As they entered her apartment, she remembered how hard he'd been to remove last time he was here. She set Copper down and went to the kitchen, where she got him some fresh kibbles. Griffin followed her.

"You look like you're wound up tighter than a broken watch. You said something about wine?"

Her hands were folded into fists and her jaw was clenched. The veins in her neck were probably sticking out. She tried to relax. Why had she offered him wine? She wanted to smack her forehead for giving in to that impulse, but she couldn't renege on the offer now.

Griffin pulled out a stool from her kitchen island and made himself comfortable as she went to the fridge and pulled out an open bottle of Chablis. "I hope white's okay."

"Sure, fine."

She got some glasses and poured the wine, then she pulled out her own stool a healthy distance from his.

"So tell me what exactly the caller said." His voice was gentle.

She could see how easily an unwitting source could spill her guts. Leo Simonetti would probably trust this guy with his secrets. So she began cautiously, reporting the conversation as accurately as she could.

"And he disguised his voice somehow?"

"With a synthesizer," Raleigh said.

"So it could be someone you know," Griffin said, "worried that you might recognize his voice."

She took a sip of the wine, cold and crisp on her tongue. "I hope you're wrong."

"What was his attitude? Did he seem scared? Crazy? Angry?"

"Angry," Raleigh said. "But very confident. I got the feeling nothing I said would shake this guy." She paused, unfocusing her eyes, trying to grab on to something, a memory, a feeling…

"What?" Griffin asked.

She was reluctant to say.

"Whatever it is, spit it out. We're brainstorming here."

"My father-in-law," she finally said. "He's a lawyer himself, and one of the few people in the world who intimidates me."

"You think it could be him?"

She listened to the voice in her mind once again, then shook her head. "I couldn't say. He never cared for me—neither of Jason's parents thought I was good enough for their son. But after the accident, things got ugly."

"That was several years ago, though."

She nodded.

"Has anything happened recently that involved them? Any legal issue, anything regarding your husband's estate?"

"I don't think—" Wait. There was something. "Just a second." She hopped off her stool and headed for her home office, where she dealt with mail and bills.

Yes, here it was, a letter from a lawyer regarding

a life insurance policy. It was a small policy she and Jason had taken out when they got married.

She brought it into the kitchen and handed it to Griffin. He read it, then looked up. "So this annuity couldn't be cashed in until now?"

"I guess that's what it means. It's only seven thousand dollars. John Shinn wouldn't care about such a paltry sum."

Griffin wasn't so sure. "Who would be the secondary beneficiary of this policy?"

"Jason's parents, I'm sure."

Griffin tapped the letter on the counter. "Just exactly how ugly did things get between you and them?"

Raleigh took a deep breath. "Extremely. At the funeral, John Shinn slapped me in the face."

"Look, I'm sorry, I don't mean to bring up painful memories for you. But it sounds like your father-in-law has a temper and might be prone to violence." He tapped the letter again. "What we have here is a motive. The insurance thing could have stirred up some old emotions—very potent, and possibly deadly."

## CHAPTER FIVE

GRIFFIN DIDN'T WANT to scare Raleigh. Hell, she'd
been shaken enough when she'd gotten the call. When
she'd grabbed her dog and headed for home, her body
language had alarmed him enough that he'd revealed
his presence to her.

But neither did he want her to underestimate the
threat.

The size of the annuity was immaterial—people
killed for fifty dollars. The idea that Raleigh might
profit from her husband's death could have sent Jason's father over the edge, from ugly to criminal.

It was just a theory, but one that ought to be looked
into.

Griffin also couldn't rule out that Raleigh had
faked the phone call to make herself appear more like
a victim. She might have spotted his car and launched
her dramatic act. A courtroom lawyer like Raleigh
would be well versed in theatrics. He couldn't let her
beautiful face—and she was beautiful, even if she
tried to hide the fact—distract him into dumping his
reporter's skepticism.

"My father-in-law doesn't have any connection to

Anthony Simonetti," Raleigh pointed out, her voice stronger now. "The phone call I received doesn't really fit."

"Could be a smoke screen. After all, the caller doesn't want to broadcast his identity to you."

Raleigh shivered. "I hate this idea. Let's not jump to any conclusions. The caller could be a lot of people."

Griffin frowned. "Like who?"

"Anyone who wants to see me and/or Project Justice go down. It could be someone from the victim's family. After his arrest, Michelle Brewster's family was very vocal in their desire to see their daughter's killer executed."

"People do a lot of not-nice things in the name of grief," Griffin agreed. "Do you think a cop or a lawyer could be responsible? They arrest criminals and get them convicted, you put them back out on the street."

"A few of them do resent us. I wouldn't rule it out."

Griffin hesitated to voice his next thought. But it had to be said. "What if our perpetrator is the real murderer? Because *someone* shot Michelle Brewster. And if Anthony is innocent, as you believe, the gun could point right to the guilty party. That would explain both the frame and the call."

Raleigh set down her wineglass. "So the real murderer tries to discredit me, disrupt my case, distract me and scare me so I can't do my job. Plus, the police think I'm a cheat or in cahoots with organized crime figures, and they ignore me."

"It could get worse than that, Raleigh. We could be dealing with a cold-blooded murderer. He's not someone to underestimate."

She nodded, looking more and more uncomfortable as the conversation progressed.

"Any problems on the job? Professional rivalries, jealousies—"

"No." She didn't hesitate about that answer, he noticed. "Although I don't have a lot of close friends at the office, we all respect and admire each other. It's the best place to work I can imagine."

Griffin wouldn't know. His world was fraught with jealousies and backbiting, sniping and passing the buck. Reporters vied for the same job, like he and Paul Stratton. Even within his own organization, he was constantly competing with other reporters over hot stories, the best beats, and story placement within the newspaper.

"I don't know what I would have done if Daniel hadn't come along when he did. I was struggling, trying to find a job, getting into financial hot water—"

"Wait. Wasn't your husband…I mean, didn't he come from a wealthy family?"

"He did. But everything he had was in trust so nothing went to me when he died except a few personal belongings. His parents made sure of that. Daniel gave me a chance no one else was willing to. He handpicks every single person who works there. If anyone at work had a problem with me, they wouldn't handle it with an anonymous smear campaign. Trust me on this."

He would. Daniel Logan might be a good judge of character, but so was Raleigh. Her work depended on knowing whom to trust, and she was good at her work.

"Maybe I should call the police after all," Raleigh said. "At least there would be a record of what's going on. If things escalate, I mean."

He wished she wouldn't. The moment she made an official police report about the threats, her situation became a public record, and he no longer had an exclusive. But if Raleigh was in danger, the police should know.

Raleigh pulled her cell phone out of her pocket, but she hesitated before dialing. "If the police get involved, this guy might back off."

"That would be a good thing…wouldn't it?"

"I want to find out who it is!" she said passionately. "Otherwise, he'll always be a threat to me."

"I'd like to get my hands on the guy myself."

Raleigh took off her glasses, which left a red mark on the bridge of her nose. She massaged the area briefly with thumb and forefinger.

"Why do you wear those glasses?" he asked suddenly.

"Um…so I can see?"

"You used to wear contacts. Those pictures in the living room—no glasses."

"Very observant of you." She shrugged. "Glasses are less trouble, and they make me look smarter. That helps in the courtroom."

"They're also easy to hide behind. You go to a lot of trouble to make sure men don't notice you."

"Is that any of your business?" she asked sharply.

"Maybe not. But reporters are naturally curious. Other men might not look past the frumpy lawyer facade, but I have. You're a beautiful woman, Raleigh. Why don't you let the world see that?"

As he'd spoken, her eyes had grown wider and wider. He fully expected hot denials to follow. Then she would throw him out, call the police to deal with her unseen enemy, and that would be that. Sometimes his runaway mouth got him in trouble.

But she didn't deny anything. The anger he saw reflected in her eyes gradually receded, replaced by a look of perplexity, her brow furrowed, her luscious lips, moist from the wine, parted slightly.

Griffin touched her chin with one forefinger, leaned forward and did what he'd been thinking about since walking through the front door.

Funny, when he kissed her he could almost taste the surprise on her lips along with the wine. She didn't resist, didn't pull away, but neither did she soften or close her eyes.

As much as he wanted to continue, this wasn't working. He broke contact, backed off slightly.

"I guess you didn't want that," he said ruefully. Women had turned him down before, but never quite like this.

In answer she threw her arms around his neck and renewed the kiss, and this time he was the one who sat there in stunned surprise.

But not for long. He wrapped his arms around her lithe body and kissed her back, matching her fervor. Her mouth was warm and hungry beneath his, and her whole being seemed to vibrate with the power of her response to him.

It was the best kiss ever, sexy and unbearably sweet at the same time, and it ended far too quickly. Raleigh broke it off, backed away until she ran into the stove, and looked at him as if he were an unwelcome alien being that had just materialized in her kitchen.

Talk about mixed signals. He had to say or do something fast, because this meeting was going south.

"Just tell me, Raleigh," he said gently. "You want to forget this ever happened, it's forgotten. But I think it'd be a shame." He would enjoy loosening up the straitlaced attorney—fogging up her glasses, pulling the hairpins out of her bun and watching her hair fall to her shoulders and beyond, taking off that suit of armor one piece at a time. But only if it was something she wanted.

He wasn't into making women feel uncomfortable, and that was exactly what he'd done.

His words seemed to reassure her. She lost that cornered-bunny look and relaxed a fraction. "Yes, please, *please* can we forget this ever happened? I don't blame you, because you only did what I was thinking about. But I was letting the wrong part of me do my thinking."

He nodded, disappointed. "It's forgotten. But could you at least tell me why?" He picked up her wineglass and extended it. "Finish your wine."

Cautiously, she resumed her seat at the island and accepted the glass, taking a big swallow of the pale liquid.

"I had my one great love," she said wistfully. "He meant everything to me. No one could ever replace him in my heart."

He hadn't asked for her love; he'd merely wanted to explore what they could have together on a physical basis, become friends and lovers and see where it led.

But now he knew how erroneous his thinking had been. Raleigh Shinn was not a woman who engaged in casual affairs. If she ever decided to take on a lover—and that was a big "if"—she would do so deliberately, after due consideration. The relationship would be serious and committed from the get-go.

But even that would never happen if she continued to worship her dead husband. What mortal man could compete with St. Jason?

He wisely decided not to voice his opinion, which would have landed him on his ass on the sidewalk.

Griffin hoped her grief would ease up someday, allowing her to have another serious relationship, maybe another marriage. But it wouldn't be with him. He wasn't the serious, committed, true-love type. Maybe when he was more settled in his career, but not now.

"Fair enough. Friends?" He thought about extending his hand, then decided touching her in even the most innocent fashion was a bad idea.

She nodded. "Friends. But I think you should leave now."

"What about my story?"

"I don't want the whole world reading about my problems. I can't stop you from writing a story, but I hope you'll use some discretion. And that you'll keep in mind that with anything you write, our shared enemy might react negatively to it."

"Meaning he might escalate. Raleigh, I won't do anything to put you in danger, okay?"

"Thank you."

As he rode down the elevator, Griffin knew he'd lied to her. Not about the story—he wasn't ready to write it, anyway. But about that kiss… It was nowhere near forgotten, and it never would be.

RALEIGH HAD MAINTAINED her calm exterior when she'd seen Griffin to the door. Once he was gone, that all dissolved. She didn't even make it the sofa. She sank to floor right where she stood, sliding her back against the wall, and rested her forehead on her knees as her eyes burned with unshed tears and her throat constricted.

What had she done?

All these years, faithful to the memory of her husband, faithful in body, mind and spirit. Today all that had gone out the window.

She could live with the fact Griffin had kissed her. But when he'd backed off, she'd lunged for him, kissing him as if he were oxygen to a drowning swimmer. And she had wanted to do more. She still did.

Desire was understandable. She was, after all, an adult woman with all the requisite body parts and hormones. But acting on that desire, even in a small way, was not. Her whole life, she had been praised for her discipline and self-control. She was the one who stayed in her dorm room and studied while everyone else was out partying. She was the one who held her tongue around her in-laws, refusing to rise to the bait they cast again and again, trying to prove to their son she was unworthy.

She was the one who saved her money, who

eschewed instant gratification in favor of a sound retirement plan.

Yet she'd just let herself practically jump the bones of the first handsome man to show any interest in a very long time.

After sitting on the floor sobbing like an idiot for a couple of minutes, Raleigh pulled herself together. This was ridiculous. She hadn't had sex with Griffin, after all; she'd merely kissed him.

She pushed herself to her feet and walked purposefully to the table where she displayed Jason's pictures and a few of the mementos that were important to them as a couple. Jason smiled back his perpetual smile. He had always smiled. He'd been the happiest, sunniest person she'd ever known, and he'd never expressed a moment of disapproval about anything she did.

But if he could see her now...

She picked up one of the framed photos—the one she liked best. They'd been on their honeymoon in the Florida Keys, enjoying a fresh fish dinner at a seaside café. The sun was setting, and she'd said something to make Jason laugh just before snapping the picture. He looked tan and carefree.

Simply looking at that picture could conjure the smell of the ocean, the call of seagulls, the lemon and spices of the snapper she'd eaten that night.

Closing her eyes, she tried to bring those sensations back now. She couldn't.

She was losing him. Little by little, the memories were slipping away. After his death, she had spent hours writing down as much as she could remember, wanting to hold on to every single piece of their lives together. Now she knew that was impossible. She hadn't imagined she could tune him out so completely, as she had while kissing Griffin.

She hugged the photo to her chest. "Oh, Jason. I'm sorry. If you're out there watching me, you're probably shaking your head at how silly I am, trying to hold on to a marriage that ceased to exist more than six years ago."

She didn't know what else to do. Her professional life was satisfying, but as for her personal life, she had this. She didn't want another relationship, because it could only be a pale imitation of the happiness she had shared with Jason. Better to cherish her memories.

*Memories won't keep you warm on a cold winter night.*

She had no idea whose voice that was—Jason's, her mother's, maybe her own. Or Griffin's. But she wasn't going to listen. Houston rarely saw cold weather, and she had an electric blanket, just in case.

By THE TIME she arrived at the weekly staff meeting the next morning, Raleigh felt she had put things into perspective. She had lapsed, true; she'd acted impulsively and unwisely. But no one was perfect.

People had told her many times that she put too much pressure on herself. She expected the best of everyone around her, but she applied the very highest of standards to herself.

Jason had told her often enough that no human being could measure up to the bar she'd set for herself. Failing every once in a while was inevitable.

The important thing was what she did now, and she'd already plotted a course of action. She'd finally talked to Daniel late last night and told him about her mysterious enemy. He had reassured her that he would handle the situation—and it wouldn't involve contacting the police. His personal bodyguard, Randall, now shadowed her everywhere she went, and Daniel had assigned Ford Hyatt, the best investigator on staff in her opinion, to make Raleigh's stalker his priority. He would start with everyone connected to Anthony Simonetti and work outward; she had a strong feeling her enemy was somehow connected to that case.

She didn't like spending the foundation's valuable resources on a personal problem, but Daniel had insisted.

At least she didn't have to worry about Griffin anymore. She would probably never see him again. No more cozy chats. No more shared glasses of wine. And certainly no more kisses. She couldn't stop him from writing about the plot to ruin her, but she'd known going in that he might choose to write a story that didn't flatter her or Project Justice. Daniel had said not to worry about things beyond her control.

"Raleigh," Daniel said, snapping her back to the present. The entire Project Justice senior staff was assembled in the conference room; Daniel appeared on a TV screen via video conferencing. She had met the man only a few times in person, as he rarely left his estate. But somehow he managed to stay closely involved in every case the foundation handled.

"Yes, Daniel?"

"You've been awfully quiet today. What's the status of the Simonetti case?"

"I'm waiting on lab results for the gun. Once we prove it's the murder weapon, I'm hoping we can trace it to the real murderer. I should hear something any day."

"Excellent."

Raleigh quickly went over two other cases she was working on, neither as high profile or complex as the Simonetti case. She thought the meeting was about to adjourn, but Daniel summoned the group's attention once again.

"I want everyone to be on their guard. Someone is out to undermine our efforts. They started by attempting to engineer some slander against Raleigh, then escalated to personal threats."

All eyes turned to Raleigh. Among her coworkers she saw shock and concern.

"I know all of you are committed to urgent cases,"

Daniel continued, "but Raleigh is one of our own. I've assigned Ford to spearhead an investigation into these threats. If he calls on any of you for assistance, I want you to make his request a priority."

"Whatever you need," said Joe Kinkaid, who had recently been promoted to senior investigator.

"Anything, anytime," Beth said.

The others around the table echoed Joe's and Beth's sentiments, which brought tightness to Raleigh's throat. They were treating her like family, even though she kept most of them at arm's length.

Trusting Daniel had been the right decision. He'd taken the bull by the horns.

"I'm sorry to have brought this trouble into our bosom, so to speak," she said. "I know we all have more important things to deal with—"

"Nothing is more important than the safety of my people," Daniel said fiercely. "Nothing. And you're not responsible in any way, so let's stop the 'I'm sorry' business right now."

Raleigh nodded, looking down at her lap so no one would see her eyes shining with tears. She loved working for an organization that valued its employees so much.

"Now, one more item of business. There's a reporter for the *Telegram,* Griffin Benedict. He seems determined to write a story about Raleigh and these actions taken against her. Our perpetrator deliberately involved Benedict, so he already knows just about everything we know."

"Can you stop him from writing the story?" asked Beth.

"No. Although I have friends in high places, even I can't censor a major newspaper. But I'm not sure I want to."

His statement was met with surprised silence. Daniel had made it clear he mistrusted the media almost as much as he did law enforcement.

"Project Justice gets its share of publicity, mostly the sensational kind. Our work gets written up in bits and pieces. I'd like to see a more comprehensive article, or a series of articles, written about the foundation. And I couldn't handpick a better reporter for the job than Griffin Benedict. He's smart, and thorough, and balanced. I like his work."

Raleigh stiffened, and the warmth around her heart dissipated. Griffin had been talking to Daniel? How had the reporter gotten access? Daniel never, but *never,* talked to the media.

"Griffin wants to write about Project Justice from the standpoint of the danger involved in our work, building the piece around Raleigh's situation as well as other recent incidents."

"You mean Robyn," Ford said. Robyn was his fiancée, but she'd first been his client, and she'd been kidnapped when Ford's investigation had backed a criminal into a corner.

"Yes, and a few other incidents. I think it's a good angle. I'm inclined to believe the story would be generally positive. Good press is vital to our work. The more people understand what we do, the more cooperation we get."

"And the more donations we get." This came from Rachel Nieves, who headed up the foundation's fundraising efforts.

"So that Griffin can do the best job possible," Daniel continued, "I'm going to allow this man access to our offices—and to all of you. I expect you to give him your full cooperation. There will be privacy issues, of course, and we'll deal with those as they come up."

Raleigh couldn't believe this. "You're giving him full access?"

"He's not a security risk, in my opinion," piped in Mitch Delacroix. "I've done a thorough background check on him." For her benefit. She wondered if he'd mentioned that to Daniel. "Aside from a lot of speeding tickets, and a questionable stint writing for *Soldier of Fortune* magazine, he's clean as a whistle."

"He's determined to write a story about this matter, one way or another," Daniel said. "He's highly motivated to get at the truth. I would rather be on the same team with this guy—help him find the truth—than his adversary."

Ford tapped his fingers on the shiny tabletop. "You trust him?"

"As much as I trust any reporter."

Daniel trusted Griffin? "How do you even know him?" Raleigh asked.

"We spent two hours on the phone this morning. It was enough." He looked straight at Raleigh. With the life-size monitor, it was like he was in the room with them. "Raleigh, you've met him. Is there any reason we shouldn't trust him?"

Raleigh considered telling Daniel—and everyone—that Griffin had put the moves on her. Daniel would immediately call the whole thing off.

But she couldn't bring herself to raise such an embarrassing issue in front of all her coworkers. "I don't think he would publish a bunch of lies about us," she said carefully. "I mean, he could have run with the bogus information he was given about me, but he hasn't. At least, not yet. He seems interested in verifying facts."

"Good. Because you're the one he wants to shadow first. He's waiting in the lobby."

Raleigh took a deep breath. She could have gotten rid of Griffin, and she hadn't. What did that say about her and her commitment to avoid letting him into her life?

"Oh, go on, you did not get shot in the ass." Celeste, the receptionist, actually giggled, a strange sound coming from a woman well into her seventies.

Griffin reached for his belt. "Wanna see?"

Celeste shrieked with laughter again, but she sobered quickly, and Griffin saw why. Raleigh was headed for them, looking like she wanted to spit at him.

"Oh. Ms. Shinn," Celeste said, perfectly deadpan. "Your guest here was just entertaining me with tales of his mercenary days. Do you know, I used to read his stories in *Soldier of Fortune*."

"Did you like them?" Raleigh asked, sounding surprised.

"Of course! He's going to put me in his story. Right, Griffin?"

"Absolutely. You'll be my star."

"Griffin," Raleigh said, refusing to take part in the light banter. "Daniel tells me I'm to show you around and extend every courtesy." Her tone of voice indicated she'd rather string him up and use him as a target for a spirited game of darts.

"I'm looking forward to it. But Daniel also said I shouldn't keep you from your work. I can just hang out, see what you do on a normal workday. I'll be like a fly in the wall."

"Or a cockroach," she mumbled just loud enough for him to hear. Then she continued in a normal voice. "Our staff meeting ended early. I have a few minutes. Come this way."

Raleigh led Griffin through the door in the frosted glass partition that separated the lobby from the rest of the first floor. As soon as they were out of earshot of Celeste, however, she stopped and turned on her heel to face him, breathing fire.

"I can't believe you went over my head. I told you I didn't want this story written."

"I'm not going to slam you," he said. "But I didn't get where I am by giving up on a story the first time someone says no."

"Does Daniel know you were a mercenary?" she asked suspiciously.

He grinned. "I wasn't a mercenary. That was Celeste's embellishment. I wrote stories about soldiers and wars."

"So you didn't really take a bullet in the, ah…"

"That part was real. Made for great copy."

Raleigh rolled her eyes. She shook her head and led Griffin past a bank of elevators to a large open area with a few cubicles here and there, desks at odd angles, lots of computers. Several people were either on computers, on the phone, or gathered in small groups.

"This is the nerve center of Project Justice. We have four senior investigators—I'm one of them—who coordinate anywhere from four to six cases at a time. But we have a pool of experienced people—former cops and lawyers, analysts, computer experts—we can draw from to help with legwork. Everyone who works here is handpicked by Daniel himself."

She gave him about ten seconds to observe before whirling around and heading down a different hallway, to the break room. Seemed she wanted to get the tour over with as quickly as possible.

Griffin's eyes bugged out when he saw the array of deli trays, salads, bowls of fresh fruit and chocolate available to Project Justice employees. "This certainly puts the break room at the *Telegram* to shame," he said. "I'm lucky if I can turn up scorched coffee and a stale doughnut."

Next she showed him their small laboratory. "We mostly do preliminary testing here. Anything we do has to be duplicated by a certified lab. But the results we get here often point us in the right direction."

Next stop was the boiler room, where interns and volunteers manned phones, stuffed envelopes and performed other, less glamorous, work.

"The second floor is executive offices," Raleigh explained. "The third floor is a health club and an executive lounge."

"Do you ever go there?"

"No, but I'll take you up there if you really want to see it."

"Another time. I was hoping you could answer a few questions for me."

She pointedly looked at her watch. "What?"

"Your receptionist, Celeste. Did Daniel handpick her as well?"

"Yes, he did. She's more than a receptionist. She knows everything that's going on around here, and she's quite well qualified. Forty years as a police officer."

"She's scary."

"Really? Seemed you were having a good time with her."

"I figured if I kept her laughing, she wouldn't pull any moves on me. Does she really have a black belt in karate?"

"Third degree. She claims she studied with Bruce Lee."

"I could do a whole story on her alone."

"What a great idea! Why don't you?"

"You know the story I want."

"It might turn out to be nothing. We might never hear from this guy again. Then you would have wasted all your time."

"It'll be a good story," he insisted. "I've developed a pretty good instinct for knowing when something is going to pop. Anyway, you forget—your enemy is my enemy, too. He involved me, personally. It's not something I'm just going to walk away from."

"What about your job? Don't you have other stories to write?"

He shrugged, but Raleigh's observation was on the money. He was working every free hour on the Raleigh Shinn/Project Justice story, but he'd promised the story to *Currents.* He had to produce something for his present employer.

His editor at the *Telegram* allowed him a lot of

freedom and didn't make him account for his time; he could come and go as he pleased. But he was expected to file a story at least once a week, or explain why he couldn't. Right now, he couldn't do either, which wasn't making his editor very happy. Claims of "protecting his source" only took him so far.

In truth, he didn't feel good now about offering the Project Justice story to CNI and he wished to hell he hadn't done it. He wouldn't hesitate to lie to a source if it helped him get information he needed, but he'd never fudged the facts with his own editor before, and it didn't sit right with him.

If he truly believed he could land the TV job, he would resign from the *Telegram*. But he wasn't that confident.

To assuage his guilt, he had offered to represent the *Telegram* at a press conference this morning. The governor was announcing his decision regarding running for reelection. Ho-hum—as if there were any doubt. But Griffin could eke a story out of it.

"What are your plans this afternoon?" he asked Raleigh.

"A little light reading. Still working on the Simonetti trial transcript."

He wanted to keep an eye on Raleigh, but he honestly didn't want to sit and watch her read. Without something to occupy his own mind, he would quickly turn to fantasies about her.

She must have read the disappointment in his eyes.

"This work is not glamorous," she said. "It's mostly researching, reading, talking on the phone—and thinking. Sometimes I just sit and stare at the wall, trying to figure out one anomaly. Won't make for 'good copy.'"

"You're trying to get rid of me."

"How astute of you." But after a moment, she dropped the challenging thrust of her chin and spoke to him frankly. "Look, Griffin, nothing has happened since the phone call. I'm beginning to think it was just a…a bad joke."

Not Griffin. "We'll see. Right now, though, I have to go to a press conference. I'll be gone about three hours." That would be plenty of time to attend the event, corner the governor for some one-on-one time, and file his story.

"Take your time."

"I'll be back later. Maybe you can tell me more about the Simonetti case."

She sighed. "Okay."

"You aren't going to leave the building, are you?"

"I might. My days can be unpredictable. But don't worry—Daniel's own personal bodyguard is watching over me."

"If you do leave, be careful, all right? Do not let down your guard. That's when the worst can happen. That's not the story I want to write."

## CHAPTER SIX

AN HOUR LATER, Griffin found himself at a Sheraton Hotel, counting the minutes until he could escape. He'd worked his way up to the front of the crowd of reporters and political groupies, and he had a few questions prepared.

He'd tried to get some one-on-one time with Governor James Redmond. But Griffin hadn't been able to get past the PR woman, who'd turned him down flat.

"So, you got stuck on the boring beat, too."

Griffin whirled around and found himself face-to-face with Paul Stratton. He and Paul weren't exactly friends, but the reporting world was pretty small, and they ran into each other from time to time, even competed on some of the same stories.

He had a healthy respect for the older man, who could have settled into his cushy anchor job but instead continued to investigate his own stories, some of them pretty heavy hitting. But personally Griffin didn't like Paul much. Or maybe that was just jealousy talking. Stratton's salary was probably three times what Griffin's was.

"Sometimes you lose the coin toss," Griffin agreed amicably.

Paul ostentatiously adjusted his tie, showing off a blindingly shiny gold ring in the shape of the Pulitzer coin. Rumor was he'd had the ring designed and cast himself, so he could carry his journalistic achievement with him always.

"This story seems a bit tame for you," Griffin observed.

"Our political guy is out with the flu. Anyway, I got an exclusive with the governor a few minutes ago," Paul said smugly. "The video is already back at the station. Should be airing right about—" he glanced at his watch "—now."

Griffin struggled to control his reaction. Why had Paul gotten an exclusive, and Griffin hadn't gotten the time of day? He had assumed no one would get a one-on-one today, but apparently he'd been wrong.

Was he slipping?

No, he probably should have put in his request sooner. Guys in public office sometimes didn't like spreading themselves too thin with the media interviews.

"So why are you still hanging around?" Griffin asked, feeling uncharitable. "Sounds like you got your story."

"They always have good food at these gigs. Only way they can ensure a lot of people show up." To emphasize his point, Paul stuffed a caviar-laden cracker into his mouth. "Mmm, beluga. Higher class than normal."

Griffin wouldn't know beluga caviar from peanut butter. But Stratton came from a well-to-do Houston family and had been raised in the country-club set. Griffin wondered if Paul's family connections would tip the balance his way with CNI.

"So," Paul said, lowering his voice. "I heard you're a candidate for the open slot at *Currents*."

"Likewise," Griffin said cautiously.

"Do you know if they're considering anyone else?"

"They're keeping their cards pretty close to the vest." Griffin was wary of repeating anything he'd heard from the news network.

"If they hire you, you'd be the youngest *Currents* anchor in history."

"Really?" Pierce hadn't mentioned it, so Griffin hadn't considered his age a pro or a con.

"I'd think with the aging baby boomers, they'd want to skew their star reporters a little older. I'm sure high-school girls would tune in by the droves to see you, but little girls don't have the buying power the advertisers want."

"Maybe I should put some fake gray in my hair," Griffin said with a laugh, staring pointedly at Paul's thick, silvery cap of hair, sprayed into place no doubt. "You know, to appeal more to the Geritol set."

Paul scowled, but then quickly schooled his

features. "Don't feel bad if they pass you over. In a few years, when you've had a bit more seasoning, maybe they'll consider you again. And, hey, I could put in a good word for you at Channel 6. They'll have a vacancy."

"You're all heart, man."

The governor made his announcement in his typical boring fashion. When his handler opened the floor for questions, no one seemed to have any. Not one to ignore an opportunity, Griffin spoke up.

"Governor Redmond, what do you think about the current bid to exonerate Anthony Simonetti?"

"I think it's ridiculous," the governor said quickly. "Project Justice is wasting its time."

"No chance you would stay his execution?"

"I would have to see some pretty startling evidence to put that man on the street," Redmond said.

"Thank you." That would make for a nice sound bite if Raleigh succeeded in her quest.

Paul Stratton buttonholed Griffin as he was heading out the door. "Is that the story you're working on?" He sounded dubious.

Griffin wasn't about to share anything concerning Project Justice with the opportunistic reporter. "I saw a press release on it this morning. Just curious."

"Trust me, that story's a real nonstarter. I covered the Michelle Brewster murder. In fact, I broke the story. My reporting helped solve that case. Simonetti is guilty as hell."

"I figure he's good for it," Griffin agreed quickly. "I was just tossing Redmond a bone, giving him a chance to pontificate about his tough-on-crime platform."

Griffin felt good about Paul's attitude. If he wasn't interested, chances were no other reporters were pouncing on it, either.

GRIFFIN SHOWED UP bright and early Monday morning with a new method of torturing Raleigh—a camera.

He snapped shots of her at odd moments, always when she wasn't expecting it.

But he wasn't completely annoying. Over the weekend, he had read up on the Anthony Simonetti trial and had offered some surprisingly astute insights. He'd caught one witness in a lie, which no one else had picked up on. With Griffin's help, she had a new lead to follow.

"I thought you were going to be a fly on the wall," she said as she began packing up her briefcase. She had a deposition scheduled for later that morning.

"I thought maybe if I made myself useful, you'd want me around more. It hurts my feelings that you're trying to get rid of me."

"I'm not..." She stopped before completing the lie. Yeah, she'd been trying to get rid of him—more because he rattled her than because she was worried about the story he would write.

"You won't let me come with you for the deposition."

"Privacy issues," she reminded him.

He raised his camera and snapped three shots of her in rapid succession.

"Griffin, don't."

"Why not? You're pretty. Look." He swiveled the camera around and let her look at the screen. What she saw was a woman with glasses too big for her face and a hairstyle so severe it might have been painted on.

But he'd caught her during a moment of vulnerability. She looked...troubled. "You should erase that one."

"I like it. I'm keeping it."

The warmth in his voice sent pleasurable shivers up her spine. She purposely looked over at the picture of Jason she kept on her desk, stared at it for many seconds, until her pulse returned to normal.

It was too early to leave for her deposition, but she started gathering her things anyway. "Joe Kinkaid will talk to you this morning while I'm gone, if you like."

"Sure I can't go with you?"

"Positive."

To his credit, Griffin didn't push. "I'll see you when you get back, then."

Raleigh tried to dismiss him from her mind as she focused on the task at hand: taking the deposition of a traumatized child. It was exhausting work, teasing an incredibly painful tale from a twelve-year-old girl, a story that would exonerate her uncle, currently sitting in prison convicted of raping his niece and leaving her for dead.

By the time Raleigh returned to the office at around one o'clock, she was wrung out, physically and emotionally, and she just wanted to climb in bed and sleep for a week.

But no, she had to deal with Griffin, a man whose very presence challenged her entire being. At least she could count on some verbal sparring with him, which would distract her from the child's disturbing testimony.

"Is Griffin around?" she asked Celeste, praying he'd gotten bored with Project Justice and gone home for the day.

Celeste consulted her sign-in sheet. "Left for lunch a while ago."

She wondered who he'd gone with, and felt left out. She should have stopped for lunch herself. Maybe there was something good in the break room.

She made a side trip to her office first to dump off her briefcase and check for messages. Still returning phone calls at 1:20 p.m., Raleigh's stomach rumbled, and she became aware of a delectable scent wafting into her office. Garlic, oregano, tomato sauce… pizza?

Someone tapped on her office door, open a crack

not because she relished interruptions but to help with ventilation. "I come bearing gifts," a deep male voice informed her.

Griffin. And pizza. Was she ready for her two biggest temptations in the same room? "Come in, Griffin."

The door opened and Celeste barged in with Griffin in tow. "This handsome young man claims he has to deliver your pizza personally. Thought I better check out his story." Her eyes sparkled with humor.

*Handsome young man?* Had Celeste fallen off the deep end?

Maybe she was simply angling for a slice of pizza. Though she was thin and wiry as a bull rider, she ate like a sailor on shore leave.

"Shall I throw him out on his ear?" Celeste grabbed that ear as she said it.

"Hey, you kick me out, the pizza comes with me," Griffin protested good-naturedly.

"Better let him stay, then," Raleigh said. "Celeste, you want a slice?"

"Maybe a small one. I have to watch my girlish figure." Celeste waggled her bony hips and tossed her curly gray hair over her shoulder. Today she wore skintight black pants, a billowy shirt that looked like an old chenille bedspread, and huge dangly earrings in the shape of pink flamingos.

Raleigh cleared a spot on the coffee table in the seating area of her office, and Griffin set the box down. The pepperoni pizza was huge, plenty to share. He removed a large slice, put it on a napkin and handed it to Celeste.

"Come back for more if you want."

"I might come back, but only to flirt with you, stud-muffin."

Griffin winked at her. "Think I'm enough man for you?"

"No, but you might come close." Celeste scurried out the door, cackling with pizza in hand, leaving Raleigh to stare after her with her mouth hanging open.

"Who was that woman?" she asked. "Certainly not the Celeste I know and fear."

"She's wonderful. I must have gotten a bad first impression."

Raleigh shook her finger at him. "Everyone gets a bad first impression. Griffin, you aren't really going to write about Celeste, are you? I was kidding you when I suggested it." God knew what the general public would make of her.

"I don't know yet."

Raleigh selected her own small slice of pizza. She didn't normally indulge in anything cheesy and greasy, but it did smell good. "Clearly you've found some way to get on her good side. Frankly, I didn't know she *had* a good side."

"We talk about *Soldier of Fortune.* The woman's got an incredible memory. She actually recalls some of the stories I wrote almost word for word. I had no idea I had a fan out there from the old days."

Raleigh frowned as she picked off the pepperoni, one of the unhealthiest foods on earth. "That's odd. She's not crazy about men in general. She makes an exception for the guys who work here, but usually that means she gives them a grudging respect and not much more. She was *flirting* with you."

"I just have that effect on women." Griffin shrugged and grabbed some pizza, settling onto her small sofa to devour it, propping those scuffed ostrich-skin boots on her coffee table.

He certainly had a strange effect on *her,* but she didn't feel like agreeing with him. "Thanks for the pizza."

"How was the deposition?"

"Mission accomplished."

"And no more creepy calls from anonymous weirdos?"

"No. Randall made sure no one followed us, too. I wish we had some way to draw Mr. Creepy Caller out. I'd like to get this business concluded."

The phone on Raleigh's desk buzzed and she got up to answer it. Someone had called her direct line—they hadn't gone through Celeste.

Since they'd just been talking about creepy phone calls, she grabbed her pen and notepad, then answered with some trepidation. "Raleigh Shinn."

"Raleigh, it's Julia."

Stunned, Raleigh said nothing for a few breathless moments.

"Raleigh?"

"Yes, Julia. Sorry." Raleigh motioned urgently for Griffin to come closer. She scribbled on her pad so he could read: *Jason's mother.* "It's been such a long time, I was just surprised."

"I know, dear, we haven't kept in touch as well as we should."

Griffin leaned in closer so he could hear Julia's side of the conversation. Raleigh tilted the phone receiver out so he could hear better and tried not to think about how close he was, how she could feel his body's warmth radiating straight into her, to her core.

Raleigh considered and rejected a number of retorts. Why would she want to keep in touch with a woman who had openly accused her of killing her son? Of being a gold digger? Who brazenly defied her son's wishes so that his widow would have to struggle?

But if the elder Shinns had anything to do with the threats, she needed to find out, and that meant keeping the lines of communication open. What a coincidence that Julia would contact her now, of all times.

"I wanted to let you know that John is in the hospital," Julia said. "He's had a heart attack."

"I'm sorry to hear that." Raleigh's voice warmed

slightly. Whatever awful things the woman had done, if her husband's life was in danger, she was probably scared and hurting. Hard to picture, though. Raleigh had seldom seen any emotions from Julia other than anger when she didn't get her way, and smugness when she did. "Is it bad?"

"Bad enough. He'll have coronary bypass surgery tomorrow. But for now, they say he's out of immediate danger."

"That sounds promising. Hopefully they've caught it in time."

"I dearly hope so. I'm calling you because…well, because John has asked to see you."

Raleigh couldn't have been more surprised if Julia had announced they'd put her in their wills. She didn't really want to see her father-in-law. Face-to-face, it was hard for her to be civil, though maybe she could hold her tongue in a hospital setting.

"He's at Johnson-Perrone," Julia said.

Griffin turned to face her head-on, nodding vigorously. *Say yes,* he mouthed.

"I can come this evening." It was all Raleigh could do to drag the words out.

"That would be fine."

"Do you know why he wants to see me?" she asked.

Julia hesitated. "I'm not really sure. Well, you must be busy. We'll see you tonight."

Raleigh blew out a breath and put down the receiver.

"Interesting," Griffin commented, putting a safe distance between them, *thank God*.

"No kidding." Raleigh made a quick notation of the call, date, time and what was discussed. "I haven't heard a peep out of them in all these years, and suddenly they turn up like a bad penny—just when I suspect they might be involved."

"It's that insurance policy," Griffin said. "You watch. They'll bring it up within five minutes of your arrival."

"I take it you don't think people can change?"

"People *can* change," Griffin said. "But it's not the first explanation I look for when someone acts weird."

## CHAPTER SEVEN

A KNOT OF DREAD formed in Raleigh's stomach as the Bentley moved closer to Johnson-Perrone Medical Center, on South Main Street near the Loop. Randall was at the wheel—did the man ever get time off?—and Griffin sat beside her, but she still felt very alone.

Was she about to face someone who despised her so much that he would try to ruin her completely? If the Shinns still held her responsible for Jason's death—and how could they not?—she supposed their hate could run deep.

Griffin kept shooting concerned looks at her. He hadn't asked permission to come with her. He'd simply followed her to the garage, where Randall had parked the Bentley to wait for her. In truth, she wanted someone with her as a witness. Jason had never spotted his parents' venom, but surely an impartial journalist would see it.

"How long did you say it's been since you've seen your in-laws?" he asked when the silence between them had dragged on a long time.

"I checked my calendar this afternoon. It's been

almost five years. It was at a lawyer's office, signing away every penny of Jason's estate."

"How could they do that?"

"I told you, they couldn't stand me. Julia called me an emotional cripple."

"Why, in God's name?"

"Because...I have severe night blindness. She was sure I made it up because I wanted Jason at my beck and call, driving me here and there in the evenings."

"Did he allow his parents to abuse you?"

"Jason didn't know the extent of it. They kept things light in front of him."

"Why do they hate you so much?" Griffin sounded bewildered. "I understand they thought you shouldn't inherit from his estate. That's not an uncommon attitude with wealthy families. They like to keep the money in the hands of blood relatives. But you didn't fight them for the money, right?"

"No. I didn't fight for anything, though I probably should have. I wasn't capable at that time. I've never asked for money. There was more involved."

"What, exactly?"

Raleigh took a deep breath. "Off-the-record, okay?"

"Can't do it, Raleigh."

"But you won't print this unless the Shinns turn out to be the bad guys, right?"

He nodded his agreement. "That's a fair compromise."

Griffin waited, and Raleigh made the decision to tell him the whole truth. Maybe he would have some insight she lacked. "They blame me for Jason's death."

"What? He died in a car accident, right?"

"Yes. But I was driving. At night. I should never have gotten behind the wheel after dark."

"Why didn't Jason drive?"

"He did drive, on the way to the event. We were attending a charity art auction that benefited a crime victim's fund, and it was important to me. He hated those black-tie events and would never have gone, except that I couldn't drive myself. He spent the whole evening at the bar."

"He drank too much?"

"Yes. I mean, he wasn't falling down drunk, but he'd had a few. I figured between the two of us, I was less impaired. Stupid, stupid. Should have just called a cab, but he didn't want me to. I knew the way, I thought I could handle it. But I must have taken a wrong turn. That road where we wrecked—it wasn't on the route."

"You don't remember?"

She shook her head. "I don't remember anything beyond getting into the car. The next thing I recall, I'm in a police car." Unfortunately, that scene she remembered with crystal clarity—sitting in the back of a squad car with a blanket draped over her shoulders. She'd been wet, shivering, barefoot, her stockings torn, Jason's blood all over her dress.

"That's awful. I'm sorry."

"John and Julia blamed me from the beginning, of course. How could they not? It was a bad judgment call on my part," she said in a small voice.

"Maybe. But that's no excuse to treat you like dirt," Griffin said fiercely. "It was an accident."

"We wouldn't have been on the road at all if I hadn't wanted to go to the stupid auction," she said wearily. "It was cold and wet, and we should have anticipated the roads might be bad. I should have stopped Jason from drinking—we should have gotten on the road sooner. According to them, my sins were many."

"Good God, you aren't buying into that crap, are you? Your husband is the one who chose to get drunk when he knew he was supposed to drive you home."

"Of course I don't buy into it," she said hotly. "I'm just explaining how my in-laws think of it. After Jason's death I became 'that woman,' and they couldn't get rid of me fast enough. They shut me out from all sorts of decisions, including the details of his funeral, and I was so shell-shocked I just went along with whatever they said. Then they gave me thirty days to vacate the apartment we'd lived in—the lease was in the name of Jason's trust. So I packed my things and moved out."

"That's criminal," Griffin said fiercely. "You were a grieving young widow, you'd just lost everything, and they kicked you to the curb?"

"It all seemed perfectly reasonable at the time."

"Well, it's not reasonable. Why do you give them the time of day? I'd have hung up on the woman when she called today."

"Julia must be devastated. I can't turn my back on that. Anyway, they're Jason's parents. Whatever their faults, he loved them. I will treat them with respect to honor him."

Raleigh could tell she hadn't justified her actions in Griffin's eyes. His lips were firmed into an angry line.

"Okay, so maybe I agreed to see them tonight because I'm a little curious. Part of me keeps hoping they'll have had a change of heart, that they'll realize how harsh they were, and reconsider."

Raleigh didn't really believe that would happen. But hope sprang eternal.

"It'll be a quick visit," she said, hoping to nudge Griffin out of his disapproving mood. "I'll find out what John wants, wish him a speedy recovery, and get the hell out of there."

A muscle jumped in Griffin's jaw.

"They can't take anything else from me," she said in a low voice. "If they could expunge Jason's memories from my brain, they'd probably do that. But they can't."

"Judging from what they've already done...I wouldn't underestimate them."

GRIFFIN COULDN'T DENY his own curiosity about Raleigh's in-laws. They sounded like greedy, horrible people to him. The research Griffin had done so far indicated that John Shinn was a vicious corporate attorney who specialized in victimizing ailing companies. He had a knack for keeping them out of bankruptcy while he lined his pockets, eventually leaving behind an empty shell of a business.

Julia was a prototypical corporate wife who filled her days with charity work, clubs, and weekly trips to a pricey salon. She was often mentioned as a crackerjack fund-raiser, a good administrator on the boards of a dozen charities.

No one mentioned her warmth or her humor or her kindness or compassion, which suggested to Griffin that she lacked those attributes.

As Randall pulled their car into the hospital parking lot, Griffin spotted a Channel 6 news van, and his internal antenna flickered to life.

"Wonder what that's about?" Raleigh asked, sounding not that interested.

Randall got out first and opened Raleigh's door while Griffin let himself out and marched ahead, curious about the TV van but not wanting to show it.

He reached the edge of the small group of curious onlookers. A male reporter had a microphone stuck in the face of an attractive older woman. *Attractive* meaning well put together—perfect clothes, salon-fresh hair, long, polished nails. But she looked too "well preserved" in Griffin's book, a hard woman with a too-thin, rigid body, stiff hair and a fake, toothy smile.

The reporter, Griffin realized with a start, was Paul Stratton. And the woman…oh, hell, Griffin recognized her from pictures he'd seen.

Randall and Raleigh caught up with him. "Are you coming with us or—" Raleigh cut herself off. "Oh, my God. That's *her.*"

"I know."

"His condition is stable," Julia Shinn was saying to the TV camera, with just the right catch in her voice. "I have every belief he'll come through the surgery with flying colors. John is a fighter. And he'll fight the charges against him. He's innocent, and we intend to prove it."

Griffin gauged Raleigh's response; she looked as surprised as he was.

"We should get out of this open area." Randall stood behind them, holding the small flower arrangement Raleigh had insisted she had to buy on the way to the hospital. He was always unfailingly polite with his requests, but the authority in his voice made everyone—even Griffin—want to do exactly as he asked.

"Let's go," Raleigh said to Griffin. "Before Julia—"

"Raleigh, there you are!" Julia practically shrieked. She ran over and threw her arms around Raleigh. "I'm so glad you're here." She released Raleigh and faced the camera, which had quickly swiveled to follow the action. "This is my daughter-in-law, Raleigh."

Raleigh, probably accustomed to TV cameras, quickly schooled the shock from her face.

"Raleigh Shinn, from Project Justice," Paul said for his viewers' benefit. "Do you have any comment regarding the fraud charges against your father-in-law?"

"No comment. I'm not here in any professional capacity." She deftly turned and allowed Randall to usher her away from the cameras.

"I'll catch up in a minute," Griffin murmured to her as she brushed past him.

"Thanks, Mrs. Shinn, for the interview," Paul said in his kindest, most compassionate voice.

"I'm happy to talk more once my husband's health has improved," Julia said. "We have nothing to hide." She followed the same path Raleigh and Randall had taken.

That was when Paul glanced over and caught sight of Griffin. He wandered over, wearing a frown, as his crew began packing up their equipment. "I might have known I'd find you here. Looking for crumbs?"

"In all honesty, Paul, I'm not here as a reporter. I'm visiting a sick friend." His words sounded phony even to Griffin. "What the hell is going on?"

Paul shrugged theatrically. "It'll be on the ten-o'clock news."

"C'mon, Paul, just tell me. It's not my kind of story."

Paul seemed to consider, then finally dropped his guard. "You'll hear about it soon enough. John Shinn is facing federal charges—embezzlement, fraud, tax evasion. Got caught bilking his own law partners for millions. Rumor has it he's some kind of gambling addict."

Griffin wondered how the Shinns' sudden financial woes might play into the threats against Raleigh. If the Shinns suddenly found themselves short on funds, it might make sense that they would try some ploy to bleed more out of Raleigh. As if they hadn't taken enough from her.

But what was their ultimate plan? Would they get the life insurance benefits if Raleigh was in jail? If they had money woes, they wouldn't deposit twenty grand in Raleigh's account…unless they were sure of getting it back after it had done its job, making it appear Raleigh had taken a bribe.

He burned every time he thought about anyone trying to hurt her.

Funny, only a few days ago he'd wanted to nail Raleigh Shinn to the wall. Now, he was protecting her, and not strictly for the sake of his story. She'd gotten under his skin, and he'd better be careful or he would lose all objectivity.

"Thanks, Paul."

"You owe me one."

"You're going to recommend me for the Channel 6 anchor job, remember?"

Paul flashed a grin. "That's right."

When hell froze over.

Griffin caught up with Raleigh and Randall in the hospital lobby, where Julia was talking animatedly to them.

"I'm holding up as well as could be expected," she said melodramatically.

Raleigh made quick introductions to Griffin and Randall, describing them as "friends."

Julia eyed them both with a speculative gleam in her, then nodded. "Pleased to meet you," she said curtly, then returned her attention to Raleigh. "Well, I'm sure you want to see John." She hustled them toward the elevator. "Seeing you will cheer him up. You've always been such a favorite of his."

She spoke too loudly for a hospital setting—in case other reporters were lurking around, Griffin was willing to bet.

The elevator doors opened onto the fifth floor, which housed the Cardiac Intensive Care Unit. As soon as they all got off, Julia leveled her gaze at the two men. "This is a private family moment," she said. "I'm sure you understand."

Randall nodded deferentially. "Of course."

Though Griffin dearly wanted to listen to the conversation that went on between Raleigh and her father-in-law, the hospital staff probably wouldn't allow him in, since he wasn't family. So he didn't push.

Raleigh gave him a nod. "I shouldn't be long."

"Take your time." He watched as Julia led Raleigh around the nurses' station toward one of the ICU cubicles, which were all made of glass so the nurses could monitor the patients visually as well as through the various machines they were hooked up to.

As soon as the women were out of earshot, Griffin met Randall's gaze.

"That was interesting," Randall said.

Griffin could see all three Shinns through the glass. It appeared Julia was doing most of the talking. Raleigh's back was to Griffin, but her body language said it all. She was angry.

Griffin felt himself bristling like a porcupine. Every cell in his body urged him to barge into the cubicle and rescue her.

But common sense prevailed. First, the nurses would stop him from getting anywhere near their patient. Second, Raleigh was not a woman who typically needed rescuing. She might be angry, but she could take care of herself. She was no longer that scared young widow, paralyzed with grief.

*Stick it to 'em, Raleigh.* He hoped she wouldn't take any crap from them just because they were in a bad situation at the moment.

RALEIGH COULD NOT believe her ears. "*The family should stand together? Is that what you just said?*"

"That's exactly what I said." Julia stared at Raleigh as if she were insane. "Is something wrong with that?"

"Where was all this family solidarity when Jason died, Julia? I tried my best to draw close to you. I thought Jason's death might at least bring us all together. But you wanted nothing to do with me."

"Now, Raleigh," John said in a placating tone, "I'm sure it must have seemed that way to you. But you were oversensitive at that time in your life, and you tended to take everything we said or did the wrong way."

"There is no way I could misinterpret the words *murderer* and *gold digger,* which is what you called me."

"Now, Raleigh, don't get worked up," Julia said in a patronizing tone.

"You could pull that crap when I was young and terrified, but not now. You always thought I was toxic to your son. But the night he died convinced you once and for all. You said I killed him."

"Now, honey," John said. "We might have overreacted some, too. Losing our only child was a terrible blow."

"Yes, but you didn't seem to realize it was a blow to me, too," Raleigh said quietly. "You did your level best to sever every connection Jason and I had. You turned our friends against me, you took every material possession we owned together, and you evicted me from the apartment we shared."

"That was a financial decision by the trustee—"

Raleigh held up her hand. "Save it. I'm not going to argue with you, John, not while you're lying in ICU. You want me to tell the press we're chummy, and I'm not going to do it—because I don't lie. Anything else?"

Julia folded her arms. "Humph. You've changed, Raleigh. Who's putting these mean-spirited thoughts in your head? Is it a new boyfriend? One of those you're with, perhaps?"

"They're just friends. And it might surprise you that I am capable of independent thought."

"I should have known it was a waste of time being civil to you," Julia muttered. "You always were a common little thing, and you haven't changed a bit."

The name-calling didn't bother Raleigh. She was actually enjoying this verbal matching of wits with her mother-in-law. For once, she was holding her own. It was easy, once she started thinking of the Shinns as hostile witnesses.

She decided to go on the offensive. "So was the twenty thousand a test? Did you want to see if I'd run out and spend it on a vacation in the Riviera?"

Julia and John exchanged wary glances. "I don't know what you're talking about," Julia said.

"Sure you do. Swiss bank accounts aren't completely anonymous. Not for those who know the right people."

She'd hit her mark. Julia looked downright scared. "I think it's time you left."

"Gladly. John, for what it's worth, I do hope the surgery goes well for you and you make a complete recovery. Because I want you in perfect health when I see you prosecuted for defamation and issuing threats."

"Now, see here—"

Raleigh turned and left just as a nurse was coming in. "What are you doing in here? You've upset Mr. Shinn. His blood pressure—"

"I'm leaving."

Griffin was waiting for her near the nurses' station. "How'd it go?" he asked cheerfully.

She couldn't meet his gaze. "God forgive me, I just baited a gravely ill man."

"What?"

She didn't say anything else until they were all on the elevator. "They're facing embezzlement charges, and they were trying to play the family-solidarity card."

"Paul Stratton told me everything. Your father-in-law is in big trouble. Dipping into the till at his own law firm. Hiding assets. Probably tax evasion and fraud, as well. In short, the rest of his natural life in the state pen."

"Good heavens. I knew he was ruthless, but…no matter what he's done, I shouldn't have argued with him. I made his blood pressure go up. I could have killed him."

"You ask me, he had it coming. They invited you, remember? They baited you first. They're the ones who wanted you to pretend to be something you're not. You simply responded in kind."

"I enjoyed it a little too much."

"C'mon, Raleigh, stop beating yourself up. They're horrible people."

"Hard to believe someone as wonderful as Jason could have come from such parents." Raleigh waited until they were in the parking lot before she told Griffin and Randall about how they reacted to the mention of a Swiss bank account. "Of course they played ignorant, but they looked scared."

"So you think they're behind it all?"

She sighed. "I just don't know. It doesn't make a lot of sense. If they're trying to cozy up to me, they wouldn't want me accused of ethics violations or anything else."

"Unless we're just not seeing the big picture. Did they mention the life insurance?"

"Not a word."

So Griffin had guessed wrong. What was he missing here?

They said little on the drive back toward downtown. Randall drove them straight to Raleigh's apartment and into the garage, using the key card she'd provided.

"Are you in for the evening?" Randall asked. "Do you need me to pick up some dinner, or groceries?"

"I'm good," she said, sounding cross and not meaning to.

"Is something wrong?" Griffin asked.

"I'm sorry. It's just the stress. I'm not used to depending on anyone. Since Jason died, I've worked very hard to become independent. So it feels odd having a chauffeur-slash-bodyguard escort me everywhere." She nodded toward Griffin. "And my very own paparazzo."

"It's only for a short while," Randall said as he opened his door. "I'm sure Project Justice will solve this case."

Unless Griffin did, first.

"But what if we never do?" Raleigh said during those few moments they were alone in the car, as Randall walked around to open her door. "That's what scares me most—the idea that I might have to look over my shoulder indefinitely."

"That's not going to happen," Griffin said fiercely. "This person, whoever he is, will make a mistake. He'll go down."

Raleigh didn't know whether Griffin felt so strongly because he wanted the story, or for some other reason. But his protectiveness warmed her from the inside out. No one had cared about her welfare in a very long time.

"Thank you, Griffin." She reached over to lay her hand over his where it rested on his knee. She meant the touch only as a friendly gesture, but the voltage surged between them, forging an instant connection that felt far more than merely friendly.

Griffin's brown eyes darkened to almost black, and Raleigh inhaled sharply as memories of their kiss leaped into her mind. She wanted so badly to forget that kiss, yet the more she tried to push the memory aside, the more insistent it became.

If he had tried to kiss her again, if he had leaned forward and closed the distance between them, she would have let him. Randall, soul of discretion that he was, wouldn't bat an eye.

She could almost feel Griffin's lips on hers again, soft and warm, but demanding. Her body responded as if the kiss were actually happening, right here, right now.

But though she could see the hunger in his gaze,

he didn't kiss her. She pulled her hand away, severing the physical link, but the distance wasn't enough. She needed to get away—now.

"See you tomorrow." She grabbed her briefcase as Randall opened her door, and she practically stumbled out of the car in her haste to make her escape. Her heart didn't stop pounding until she was safely inside her apartment with the door locked.

Copper did his usual dance around her legs, so ecstatic to see her every single day. She scooped him up and cuddled him, and even let him lick her face.

Her relationship to Copper was so sweet and simple. A dog was the only animal that showed such unconditional love. Why did human relationships have to be so much more complicated?

# *CHAPTER EIGHT*

GRIFFIN FELT about as lively as warmed-over refried beans at seven the next morning. He hadn't told Raleigh, because he knew she would object, but he'd been parking outside her apartment building, watching it most of the night.

He wasn't alone. Daniel had sent a man to relieve Randall; he sat outside the building in a panel van equipped with hidden cameras. Griffin had spotted him the first night.

But it couldn't hurt for extra eyes to watch over Raleigh, right?

He didn't waste the time; he used his laptop and cell phone to research leads and ideas from the previous day. Last night, he'd gotten up to speed on the John Shinn case, reading every article that had been published and chatting up one of the *Telegram*'s business writers.

He'd also written down every license plate number of every car that entered or left the garage or pulled up to the front of the building, and he'd eyeballed every person who entered or exited the front door.

He'd even questioned the night doorman regarding

strangers, new residents or suspicious characters hanging around. But nothing unusual had popped up.

After Randall appeared at seven o'clock sharp the next morning to ferry Raleigh to work, Griffin went home, showered, and allowed himself a short nap. Lord knew she was safe at work, because no one would get past Celeste.

When he arrived at her office at around ten, Raleigh was waiting for him, dressed down—for her—in casual pants and a pale green, light cotton sweater that accentuated her deep green eyes. She'd pulled her hair back with a fancy, yellow-flowered ponytail doodad, leaving only a few strands to curl around her face—not quite as severe as her usual style.

She'd even changed her glasses from the more scholarly horn-rims to a fun pair of blue frames.

The effect was mouthwatering. Okay, so it wasn't just the prickly librarian look that drew him to her.

Last night he'd wanted to kiss her again more than anything in the world. He'd wanted to smooth those worry lines from her face and make love to her until she forgot everything but the two of them and the boundless electricity that arced between them at the most casual touch or even an exchanged glance. But given the load of guilt she'd dumped on herself after their last kiss, he'd dug deep to find some self-control.

He might be ready and willing, but she wasn't.

Even if he persuaded her to throw out her caution and have sex with him, it wouldn't end well. When Raleigh was ready to be with someone again—if ever—it would be with someone completely different from him. Someone who would love her forever.

Hell, he couldn't make promises beyond next week. His life was too unpredictable to include a regular girlfriend. If he got the job with CNI, he'd move his home base to New York. That might not be an insurmountable obstacle; long-distance romances could work. But he wouldn't stay in New York. Some hot spot or war zone or natural disaster would call his name and he'd be on a plane, failing to show up for dinner, forgetting a birthday.

He'd had girlfriends before. It never worked for long. Why that idiot local magazine thought he was an eligible bachelor was beyond him.

Raleigh's colorful glasses didn't totally hide the shadows beneath her eyes. This situation was taking its toll on her.

"You didn't sleep well last night," he said as he dropped onto her office sofa.

She gave him a disapproving once-over. "You didn't go home last night."

"How'd you know?"

"Duh. I looked out the window and spotted your car. Seriously, Griffin, what's up with that? Daniel has someone watching my place 24/7, even when I'm not there."

"If something happens, I want to be there."

"You're that worried someone will scoop you?"

It wasn't that. But he couldn't begin to explain the depth of his obsession with this story. "If it bothers you, I'll stop."

"It bothers me," she said curtly. "Wouldn't you rather be, you know, going out, doing…guy things?"

"Yeah, boy, I've really missed my usual routine, hitting the bars and strip clubs."

She peered at him over the top of her glasses. "I just assumed you have a life."

"My job pretty much *is* my life."

"Copper started barking in the middle of the night. He probably caught your scent. He's crazy about you, you know."

"Does your dog do that very often?"

"Bark in the middle of the night? No." Raleigh frowned. "He's been restless lately, though. Maybe he's just picking up on my tension, poor thing. I did see a light on across the street. Those lofts are being renovated, so they should be empty at night. But it was probably just someone working late."

Or someone casing Raleigh's building. Maybe Griffin was being paranoid, but any sort of anomaly—like a strange light or an odd person or a dog barking when he should be sleeping—bothered him.

He wished he could whisk Raleigh off to a safe house until this ugly business was over. Maybe in

Siberia. Or, even better, a tropical island. Raleigh in a bikini, her skin glistening with oil…

Ha. The chances of that were nil.

"So, how would you like to come with me to rattle a few cages at the Houston P.D.?" Raleigh had let her surly attitude slip. Her voice fairly sang with anticipation.

"I'm game. What's going on?"

"I'll tell you on the way."

A few minutes later they were once again in the Bentley's backseat.

"I got some news this morning," Raleigh began as the car pulled away from the curb. "The lab was able to fire the gun. Well, they made a casting of the barrel, then constructed a new barrel from that. Kind of the way they make a crown for a tooth. They were able to fire a test bullet. Now, the police can compare the test bullet to the bullet that killed Michelle Brewster, and we'll know if we have the murder weapon."

"Okay, I'm following so far. But what if it *is* the murder weapon? Doesn't that bolster the state's case, that Simonetti disposed of the gun quickly as he fled the scene?"

"It could. But here's the best part. The lab also was able to recover a partial registration number from the gun. Chances are very good the police can trace it to the owner. Which might lead us to the actual murderer."

"You sound pretty confident."

"I have a feeling." She glanced over, then looked down and grinned impishly. "I know, I know, that's flaky woo-woo stuff. But one of my strengths as a lawyer is that I can tell when people are lying. I have a radar for it. Most people give themselves away with subtle, physical cues. Claudia, the psychologist Project Justice consults with, has studied the science behind body language. But me, I think I've always done it on a subconscious level."

"So you've talked to Anthony Simonetti, and you believe he's telling the truth?"

"I do. I'm not one-hundred-percent accurate. I've been fooled before. Psychopaths are very good liars. But Anthony isn't a psychopath. Everyone who really knows him says he is a caring person. He had a strong relationship with Michelle. He's never been prone to violence."

"But he did work for one of his father's companies. Which means he was involved at least on the fringes of some criminal enterprise."

Raleigh sighed. "An unfortunate fact the prosecution mentioned as often as possible. Anthony did work for his father's grocery business, driving a truck. But a few months before the murder, he quit that job and broke all ties with his father. When Leo Simonetti tried to pull him into the illegal stuff, he wanted nothing to do with it. That's the reason they're no longer speaking to one another."

Griffin had to admit, Raleigh was pretty persuasive. "What do you think the cops will say?"

She sighed. "I have an appointment with Abe Comstock, the original investigator. He didn't want to see me. Doesn't want to hear what I have to say. He only grudgingly agreed to the meeting."

"If he really believes Anthony is the murderer, I'd think he'd be excited to find the murder weapon."

"He's afraid I'm right—that the gun will point to someone else."

"What will you do if he tells you to take a hike?"

She sighed again. "I can't make them reopen the case."

Maybe she couldn't. But he could. Nothing like a little bad press to nudge public officials into doing the right thing.

Randall found a place to park less than a block from the police headquarters front entrance. He fed some quarters to the meter, then he, Griffin and Raleigh headed up the front steps.

Before they'd left her office, Raleigh had added a jacket, a scarf and taller heels to her outfit. She had also slicked back her hair and replaced the fun blue glasses with her horn-rims.

"You changed your clothes," he couldn't help saying.

She flashed him a look that said she was uncomfortable. "I have to look the part."

"Ball-busting attorney?"

"Right."

Randall parked himself on a low wall outside police headquarters and lit a cigarette. Griffin and Raleigh continued inside, where Raleigh allowed her briefcase to be searched, and they both walked through a metal detector. They had to state their business at an imposing front desk manned by a stern-looking, older man in uniform. After a few minutes had passed, a young woman in civilian clothes escorted them back through a maze of corridors to the office of Lieutenant Abe Comstock.

The door was open, and the man behind the desk looked up. "Come in, Ms. Shinn." He was a good-looking guy with dark brown skin pulled tightly across sharp cheekbones, and just the beginnings of gray at his temples. He wore a suit, and Griffin was willing to bet it was tailored to fit the detective's wide shoulders and muscular arms and legs.

His demeanor was affable enough. He appeared relaxed, smiling slightly as he extended his hand.

"Thank you for seeing me so quickly," Raleigh said, shaking the man's hand. "This is Griffin Benedict, an associate who's helping me."

Comstock froze halfway into a handshake. "Griffin Benedict, the *reporter?*"

"That would be me." Griffin kept his tone friendly.

Comstock was no longer relaxed or cordial. "What do you mean, bringing a reporter to this meeting? If you think you can pressure me—"

"No, Lieutenant, it's nothing like that," Raleigh broke in hastily.

"Then what's he doing here?"

"I'm writing an overall story about Project Justice," Griffin explained, "focusing on the personalities. I'm shadowing Raleigh so I can understand what her day-to-day activities are." That sounded bland enough.

Comstock wasn't buying it. He ignored Griffin, addressing Raleigh. "If you want to have a good-faith meeting with me, we talk in confidence."

Griffin tried to smooth things over. "Look, Lieutenant—"

Raleigh held up her hand, cutting him off. "Griffin, I'll handle this. Would you step out, please?"

He hated to see anyone bully Raleigh. He wanted so badly to object. His presence could help her achieve the results she wanted. But the implacable look in her eye convinced him he'd better listen to her or there would be hell to pay. She and Project Justice could withdraw their cooperation with him at any time.

"Fine. Call if you need me." He exited the office, closing the door with a bit more force than necessary.

What if Raleigh's enemy was someone within the police department? The police had a vested interest in keeping Anthony Simonetti behind bars. They didn't want to be proved wrong, their methods and competence questioned.

What if the threat to Raleigh came directly from Abe Comstock himself? He stood the most to lose. He, and the district attorney who'd prosecuted Simonetti.

Unlike John Shinn's cubicle, Comstock's office didn't have glass walls. Griffin couldn't see a thing, and he could hear only the muffled din of voices from the other side of the door.

Of course, Comstock wouldn't try anything in his own office. But Griffin listened keenly anyway, ready to barge in if he heard raised voices. No one was going to harm Raleigh on his watch, even if he had to go up against a seasoned cop who could throw him in jail on a whim.

"So what's this about?" Comstock asked.

Raleigh deeply regretted allowing Griffin to come with her to the meeting. She should have realized how it would look—like she was putting pressure on the detective before they'd even spoken. There was a time and a place for pressure, of course. But not when she hadn't even tried diplomacy, reason and common sense.

Now Comstock was on the defensive, ready for a fight.

"It's about the gun found in the water heater."

Comstock rolled his eyes. "Please. That thing was

so corroded it was about to crumble to dust. Don't try to tell me someone could make it fire."

"Not exactly." She patiently explained the process by which her lab had made the casting. "It's not a brand-new technology," she said quickly, anticipating that argument from Comstock. "It's already been used as evidence in a murder trial, so there's a legal precedent."

"You're telling me you have a bullet, fired by this replica or model or whatever you want to call it?"

"Praktech Laboratories does. I have of course maintained an immaculate chain of custody, and Praktech has an excellent reputation among law enforcement agencies including several state police—"

"Okay, I get it."

"All I'm asking is that you do a comparison. I'm sure Janet Flanders or Monty Gilliam right here in your own lab could do it."

"And if they match? Doesn't help Simonetti's case any."

Same point Griffin had brought up.

"Unless the gun can be traced to another suspect. Someone unconnected to Anthony. The lab has also brought up the serial number—all but two digits. They used seven different kinds of chemical baths including—"

"Spare me the details. Fine. Have the lab send the damn bullet, and we'll do a comparison. And we'll run the registration number. If it'll get you out of my hair."

Raleigh quickly gathered up the papers she'd been trying to show Comstock, which he hadn't even glanced at. "Thank you, Lieutenant." Now that she'd achieved her objective, she wanted out of there before Comstock changed his mind.

"Let me tell you one thing," Comstock said, still confrontational. "If that reporter writes one word about this, he damn well better mention that the Houston Police Department is bending over backward to cooperate. We have better things to do with our time and resources than chase after ridiculous conspiracy theories and ghost suspects that don't exist. And I'd think you do, too. The right man is paying the price for that murder."

Raleigh's breath caught. *The right man is paying the price for that murder.* She'd heard those exact words, and recently, too. Where had she— Oh. The anonymous caller.

The sentence wasn't distinctive enough for her to be certain. Still, was it just a coincidence that Comstock would use the identical words?

"Please," she said, wanting to end the meeting before she gave herself away. "Let me know your findings as soon as possible. Anthony's scheduled execution is only a couple of months away."

She slipped out of the office and didn't realize how upset she was until she ran smack into Griffin.

He backed up, steadying her with his hands on her shoulders. "You okay?" he asked in a low voice, since other cops and police employees could be right around the corner. "You're gasping for air like you just ran a marathon."

Raleigh put a hand to her breast, feeling her chest rise and fall. She paused long enough to take some long, slow breaths. "I'm fine. Comstock just pissed me off, that's all. Covering his butt like every other— oh, hello."

It was the woman who had shown them in. Looking as humorless as ever, she obviously had the job of seeing them out. Neither of them spoke until they were safely on the sidewalk, Randall following at a discreet distance.

"So Comstock is taking the company line? 'The right man is behind bars'?"

"Exactly." She relaxed slightly. Even Griffin had just used a similar phrase. She was worrying over nothing. "No one's willing to admit they might have made a mistake," she groused.

"No one wants to be proved wrong or incompetent or inadequate," Griffin added. "It's human nature. Once, when I was first starting out, I was accused of misquoting someone. I hadn't recorded the interview so I had no way of proving I hadn't made a mistake. The paper printed a retraction and I was fighting mad. It's an awful feeling.

"You want to know the worst part?" he asked.

"What?"

"To this day, I'm not sure I *didn't* misquote the guy. I think when someone is on slippery ground, they get even more defensive."

"No one's infallible, I guess."

"Not even you." When they reached the Bentley, Randall was there to open doors. The guy was good.

She turned to Griffin before climbing into the backseat. "What, you don't think I'm perfect?" She was teasing him, which surprised her. But he seemed to take her question seriously.

"If you have any flaws, it's that you hold yourself to higher standards than you would anyone else in the world."

"Why do people keep telling me that? High standards are a good thing." She wasn't perfect; of course she knew that. But she hadn't really expected Griffin to mention what he viewed as her shortcomings. "I hold everyone to high standards," she said when she slid into the backseat. "When you expect the best of people, they often try to give it to you."

He smiled at her, a little sadly, she thought. "Never mind. I shouldn't have brought it up."

He climbed into the backseat from the opposite side, and Raleigh picked up where they left off.

"But you did bring it up. You can't drop it now."

He frowned. "I just think you should cut yourself

some slack now and then. How long since you've taken a vacation?"

"Not that long. It was…let me see…" Vancouver. When Jason was still alive. Oh, surely she'd taken time off to do something fun since then. "I took a few days off last November."

"How much time?"

"A long weekend."

"And what did you do?"

"Why the interrogation?"

"What did you do?" he asked again.

She sighed. "I had a wisdom tooth pulled."

One corner of his mouth crooked up in a smile, but he said nothing more. He didn't have to. She'd made his point for him.

"You're not perfect either, you know," she grumbled.

"Far from it. What don't you like about me? Give me a laundry list."

"Well…" She had to think pretty hard. "You drive too fast. Jason did, too, which was exactly why I couldn't allow him to drive that night. There was ice on the road—" She swallowed a gasp. God, she'd just *remembered* something about that night.

"Raleigh?"

"A memory. Something I never knew before just now. I remember feeling the car slip on the ice…" She shivered.

"Maybe it's best if you didn't try to remember," he said gently.

Maybe. But part of her wanted to know. Had she really been at fault? Had she driven too fast, or plunged ahead when she couldn't see?

"We were talking about my faults," he reminded her.

And she'd segued—illogically—into the night her husband had died. "I don't dislike you, Griffin."

"I'm glad, because I like you. It's not often I meet a woman who challenges and excites me like you do. But you've built this brick wall around yourself. It's like…like you can't give yourself permission to enjoy life because you're a widow."

"Just stop right there. This has nothing to do with your story."

Randall glanced back at them in the rearview mirror. He seemed completely unobtrusive, but he was listening.

"I've said too much. I'm an ass, and I'll shut up now."

But now that he'd started it, she didn't want to let it go. "Just because you've spent a few hours with me doesn't give you the right to tell me how to live." Why did he have to care one way or another about her private life? It was none of his business.

She folded her arms and glared at him, daring him to continue the argument. But she knew why she was being so defensive. It was just as he'd pointed out a few minutes ago—her argument was on shaky ground.

He was right. She did hide behind her status as a young widow. She didn't allow herself to have fun, because it didn't seem fair that she should laugh or sing or love or soak up the sun or even enjoy a beautiful sunset when Jason was cold in the ground.

It hadn't seemed to matter. She'd derived a lot of satisfaction from her work, and she got affection from Copper, her one remaining living link to Jason. The thought of starting over with a new man hadn't appealed to her at all.

Until now.

BY FIVE O'CLOCK, Raleigh had a pounding headache. She didn't bother packing up any work to take home. She signed out without saying goodbye to anyone but Celeste and headed for the garage.

At the last minute, she remembered her car wasn't in the garage. Randall had brought her to work. She was supposed to notify him when she was ready to leave and give him a few minutes.

Frustrated by the added delay, she just stood there in the lobby feeling a ridiculous urge to burst into tears.

Of course, that was when Griffin appeared.

"Hey, Celeste, I brought you a cupcake."

"Griffin Benedict, you are going to make me fat!"

But she accepted the cupcake anyway. "Someone's birthday?"

"I don't know, I just spotted them in the break room. Oh, hi, Raleigh."

He'd known perfectly well she was standing there the whole time. Griffin didn't miss much, which made it hard for Raleigh to be around him, sometimes. He saw so much more than she wanted him to.

They'd parted awkwardly after returning to the office. Now that she'd cooled off, she felt badly for how she'd acted. Maybe her private life wasn't any of his business, but she sensed he wasn't merely being nosy. Against all odds, he seemed to care about her.

"Hey, Griffin."

"Is something wrong?"

"I forgot to call Randall, that's all, and now I'll have to wait for him." She took out her phone and started scrolling through her address book.

"I'll give you a ride home. My car is parked in the garage. No one will see you leaving with me. I can drive you right to your garage."

"Let him take you home, honey," Celeste said in a rare show of concern. "Any girl would be safe with him. He's a mercenary. Are you sure you're okay?"

Raleigh realized she must look in bad shape.

"A good night's sleep, I'll be fine," she said, forcing a smile. Then, to Griffin she said, "I'd appreciate the ride."

"No problem."

She waited until they were safely in his car before she spoke again. "I overreacted this afternoon. I shouldn't have gotten so angry."

"I was deliberately provoking you. You had every right."

"Why were you doing that?"

"It's like I said. I want to get to know you better."

"Why?"

"Because I'm interested in you? Like, the way a man is interested in a woman?"

"I find that hard to believe. You're one of Houston's top ten eligible bachelors, after all. You must have women beating down your door."

Griffin groaned as he expertly navigated downtown five-o'clock traffic. "Stupid article. Can you imagine what kind of woman comes after me because they see my picture in a magazine? Do you think that's my kind of woman?"

"I don't know what kind of woman would be 'your kind.' You've been seen with models and starlets."

He shrugged. "At one time, that was easy and fun. Models and actresses want to be the center of attention. So I asked them a lot of questions, and they went to bed with me."

"And now it's not so easy and fun?" She had a hard time believing he couldn't get just about any woman to go out with him.

"Going to bed with a pretty girl who wants to see her name in the newspaper—it gets old."

"So you're…trying to get me into bed?"

"I'm *interested* in you. Can't we leave it at that?"

It would be easier if she could pigeonhole him as a shallow guy interested in another conquest. She could dismiss him from her mind then.

She called Randall to let him know she'd gotten a ride home. Predictably, he wasn't thrilled. "Daniel won't like that."

"I didn't take any chances, Randall, really." Daniel would give her grief, but she'd deal with that later.

The crisp fall day had turned overcast and muggy, reflecting Raleigh's mood. It was starting to rain by the time Griffin's Mustang pulled up to her garage entrance. She gave him her pass card and they entered the garage.

"I'll go up with you," he said, "check out your apartment and make sure everything's okay."

"It's not really necessary. We haven't heard from this guy in a couple of days. Ford's investigation hasn't turned up anything. Maybe he's given up."

"Someone who spends twenty-thousand dollars on a plan doesn't give it up that easily. Humor me."

Great. Griffin would be in her apartment again, and she knew how hard he was to evict. Especially when she felt a bit lonely and, against all odds, enjoyed his company. He was the first person to challenge her on a personal level in a very long time.

"Are you always so doggedly determined about a story?" she asked.

"It could mean a huge career leap for me. Do you ever watch *Currents?*"

"On TV? Sometimes." The truth dawned on her. "You mean that's the job you're up for? Criminy, Griffin, you'd be a household name."

"Yeah, but they're waiting to see how this story comes out, and it isn't wrapping up as quickly as I hoped it would. Meanwhile, the other guy they're considering is Paul Stratton."

"The same Paul Stratton we ran into yesterday? The one who wrote all those stories about the Michelle Brewster murder?"

"The very same. He's on the air every night, reading the teleprompter about one big story after another like they were *his* stories. And you can bet the *Currents* people are watching."

This was the first time she'd seen Griffin less than arrogantly confident. He really did want the TV job, she could see that. And he wasn't so sure he'd get it.

The elevator opened on her floor. Griffin stepped out, checked the hallway, then led the way to her front door. After she used her key on the dead bolt, Griffin entered first, checking every room and closet as

Copper treated them to a frenzy of earsplitting barks, trying to get their attention.

"Place is clean," Griffin said as he scooped up the little dog and allowed it to lick his face. He laughed, and any lingering irritation Raleigh felt toward him vanished.

"Griffin...why don't you write the story now? I think Daniel would be okay with it, he seems to trust you. You can follow up as the story progresses...if it does."

"Are you that anxious to get rid of me? 'Cause if I got the job at *Currents,* I'd move to New York and I'd be out of your hair for good."

That thought didn't exactly cheer her. But she knew what it felt like to be ambitious, to want to be the very best at what she did.

"I think maybe it's time to air the story, that's all. Maybe once our guy knows we're onto him, he'll make a move. It's tedious, waiting for him."

"The moment I break the story, other reporters will be on it. And we might scare our guy into hiding. I'd rather wait until the story has a conclusion."

"Whatever you think is best—"

She was cut off as the French doors leading out to her balcony exploded in a hail of gunfire.

## CHAPTER NINE

"GET DOWN!" Griffin tackled Raleigh and threw her to the ground as glass shards and wood splinters flew across the living room. Raleigh lost count of the bullets—three, five, ten. The shooting seemed to go on and on. A lamp shattered. Bits of plaster exploded from the wall.

Then, as quickly as it had started, it stopped and a deafening silence filled the room.

Griffin was half on top of her. He already had his cell phone in his hand. "Someone is shooting at us through a window," he said, his tone urgent but the message clear.

Thank God he was doing it—she would have babbled.

"We're on the third floor, facing Texas Street." He gave Raleigh's address.

Copper whined, and Raleigh realized she was on top of him. She raised her shoulders and allowed the dog to wiggle out, then did some wiggling of her own so she could grab the dog. She didn't want Copper getting glass in his feet.

Griffin kept a protective arm around her, trying

to hold her down as he continued to speak with the 911 operator. Raleigh was pretty sure the shooting was over: whoever was behind it would be making their escape, rather than waiting for the cops to come along and catch them in the act.

But Raleigh was too numb to try to move. Instead, she lay there, feeling safe against Griffin's warm, hard body. Copper licked her ear and whined again.

"Shh. It's okay, baby." Griffin's chest rumbled as he spoke. His breath ruffled her hair. She didn't want to move.

Eventually she had to. Sirens sounded in the distance. The shooter would be long gone.

Griffin eased himself off her. "Crawl over toward the fireplace," he said. "We can wait there. It's out of the line of fire."

Raleigh did as she was told. She'd never been shot at before, so she bowed to Griffin's apparent knowledge. He claimed he'd been shot before, so he knew more than she did.

Her only other life-or-death experience, she'd gone into a fugue state.

The brick hearth of her fireplace did seem the safest place. While much of the rest of her living room was a mess of broken glass and china, splintered wood and bits of stuffing from her sofa, this corner appeared unscathed.

With one exception. Her favorite photo of Jason had been hit. He'd taken a bullet square in the face, the glass broken in a spiderweb pattern.

She reached for the photo and touched the cracked glass while she attempted to soothe Copper, who had jumped into her lap. Poor Jason.

"Yeah, paramedics too," Griffin was saying.

Paramedics? In an adrenaline daze, Raleigh looked down at herself and with a start realized she had blood on her jacket. Just the sight of the blood made her woozy.

Was she hurt? She didn't feel any pain. She put her hands to her head, then her face, then her arms…

Griffin. She was almost afraid to look over, and when she did, her head started to spin. Blood. A lot of it—on the rug, some on her sofa—and on him.

He sat on the edge of one of her chairs holding a throw pillow against his arm. His hand and the pillow were smeared with blood, his shirt was bloody. His face, though, was pale and tense with pain.

"Griffin!" Still clutching Copper in one arm, she went to him. "Are you okay? What am I saying, of course you're not okay. You're bleeding all over…."

"Sorry about your rug. And the pillow. I'll have them cleaned."

His concern was so ludicrous she would have laughed if she hadn't started to cry. The situation was too familiar. Until this moment, she had never remembered anything about the accident that killed Jason. Now, hideous images flashed through her mind. She sank to the floor next to Griffin, sobbing hysterically.

"Hey, what's all this?"

She grabbed on to his jean-clad leg and rested her cheek against his knee. "Please don't die on me, Griffin."

"I'm nowhere near dying. Everything's okay. The bullet hit my arm. Lots of blood, but no vital organs."

"I should do something. I should get you some bandages or…or apply pressure or something—" She tried to get up, but he held her next to him with a surprisingly strong grip on her shoulder, considering the injury to his arm.

"*I'm* applying pressure. Paramedics are coming. Hear the sirens?"

She did, but they weren't here yet. She clamped her eyes closed, but the awful visions wouldn't leave her alone. Jason with the car compressed around him, his head against the broken windshield. His face covered in blood.

*She tried to stop the blood, but it was like a waterfall and he wasn't talking or moving. She needed help. But she couldn't lay her hands on a cell phone, so she jumped out of the car and ran—*

*No one. The road had been deserted. She called for help until her throat was raw, then started running in her heels and her thin wool coat, slipping every few steps on the icy road surface, finally abandoning the shoes altogether and running in her stocking feet. She fell to her hands and knees, scraping the flesh from both.*

*Then, car lights, and someone wrapping a blanket around her. The warm backseat of a car, a cocoon of blessed forgetfulness...*

"Raleigh, you okay?"

Was she okay? She snapped back to the present. Jason was dead, but here was a man alive and vital who needed her help.

"I'm sorry, Griffin." She pulled away from him, despite his weakening grip on her. "Maybe you should lie down."

"I don't want to get any more of your things bloody."

"For God's sake, I don't care about the furniture!"

He didn't argue further and she helped him to the sofa, where he could at least lean back against the cushions.

"I'll get some clean towels." She forced herself to walk on wobbly legs to the bathroom and grab three bath towels from the linen cupboard.

When she returned, Griffin's eyes were closed and his hold on the pillow had slackened. Copper sat on his lap, looking worried.

"Griffin?" She yanked the blood-soaked pillow

away and wrapped one of the towels around his arm, which bore a ragged gash that continued to bleed.

"I'm still here," he said.

Someone knocked at the door and she rushed to open it. Before she could say a word, police swarmed into her apartment, guns drawn. One of them shoved her against a wall and placed his body between her and any possible threat.

"Hey, hey, it's over. The shooter is gone. Griffin—" She pointed to the sofa. "He's been shot. Someone across the street—I'm not sure what happened."

Cops yelled at each other and yammered into radios. Then, stretchers and IV bags, men and women in blue uniforms, maybe firefighters? Copper barked at them all and no doubt would have nipped at a few of them if Raleigh hadn't grabbed the dog and tucked him under her arm.

It was all such a blur. Raleigh was forced to leave her apartment and stand in the hallway with Copper while they made certain there was no further threat from the shooter. One uniformed officer asked her a bunch of questions, but all she could think to answer was, "I don't know."

The situation was so confusing Raleigh didn't know what to do or how to behave. She'd been on the fringes of terrible crimes most of her adult life, but she'd never been in the middle of one like this.

"Is Griffin okay?" she asked every person who

came out. Most of them didn't seem to know, but finally one of the firefighters came out to tell her Griffin would survive.

"He's lost some blood, but it doesn't look like the bullet broke any bones or hit a major artery," the female paramedic told her. "But he won't consent to go to the hospital. Can you change his mind?"

"What? That idiot." Here she was all bent out of shape because she thought he might die, and he was refusing help. She wanted to march right back into her apartment and give him a piece of her mind, but the cops wouldn't allow her back in. Her lovely apartment, her oasis, was now officially a crime scene.

She was shocked a few minutes later when Griffin exited her apartment under his own steam, though he wasn't moving very fast. He was shirtless, and a very large and thick white bandage decorated his left bicep.

The moment he saw her, he went to her and crushed her against him in a surprisingly strong bear hug.

"Are you okay?" he demanded.

"I'm fine." His warm, bare skin felt good against her. "It's you who got shot, in case you hadn't noticed. I hear you won't go to the hospital."

"I told them I can't leave until I'm sure you're someplace safe. I promised you, when we left your office, that you would be safe and look what happened."

She was touched by his attitude. He wasn't being a macho, bullheaded male. He was trying to keep his word to her. "You saved my life. You took a bullet for me."

"It's not like I deliberately threw myself in its path." He didn't let her go, and she didn't want him to. She would stay in his arms all night if he would let her. He was alive, he was okay.

Eventually two detectives showed up, along with a crowd of crime-scene investigators with their cameras and bags of equipment. One detective took Raleigh and Griffin downstairs to the building manager's office, then put them in different rooms. Raleigh knew this was standard procedure, but she still felt like a suspect rather than a victim.

Several minutes passed before a detective joined her for her interview. And when the office door opened, her heart sank when she saw Lieutenant Abe Comstock standing in the doorway. Why, oh why had she antagonized the man mere hours ago?

"Looks like you got yourself in a might of trouble," Comstock said as he pulled out a rolling office chair for himself, then rolled it way too close to where Raleigh sat on a small sofa with Copper in her lap.

Copper, who usually loved everyone, growled at the detective.

"You might want to back off a hair," Raleigh said. "He's upset and he might bite. Anyway, your intimidation tactics won't work with me. I use them myself."

Comstock nodded, awarding her the point, and backed away a couple of feet. "Sorry. I guess I forgot for a minute you're a crime victim here, not a hostile defense attorney. Looks like you might have ruffled a few feathers."

"You see?" She grabbed on to the thread of reasoning he'd given her. "Whoever the real murderer is doesn't want me to prove Anthony's innocence."

"I confess, this turn of events has me wondering," Comstock agreed. "But I have to consider all possibilities. Do you have any enemies, Ms. Shinn?"

Part of her wanted to hold back. Once this story broke, other reporters would be all over it, and she felt a strange desire to protect Griffin's story. He'd worked damn hard for it, after all.

But she was an attorney, an officer of the court held to a higher standard than the average citizen. Plus, she wanted the police to find the person who had tried to kill her—fast.

"Someone's been trying to ruin my reputation," she said with a sigh. And she explained about the deposit, the altered phone bill, the threatening phone call. "The phone call seems to indicate the threats are related to the work I'm doing for Anthony Simonetti. But Griffin suggested it could be a smoke screen, to hide the perpetrator's real identity and motives."

Comstock nodded as he made notes. "Now I see

why Benedict is hanging around you. This could shape up to be a real potboiler."

"Whatever his motives, I'm glad he was there," she added hastily. "He might have saved my life." Part of her wanted to believe that Griffin was with her because he wanted to be there. He'd said he liked her. But how much of that was real, and how much was due to the article he hoped to write? The deeper he got into her psyche, the more compelling he could make the story.

She'd read his work. His stories read like bestselling fiction precisely because he did such a good job with the people involved. They weren't just quotes or sources to him, they were real people with real lives.

The thought made her uncomfortable. She'd known he was using her predicament to help him get the job of his dreams, but was he using *her?*

"When can I return to my apartment?" she asked Comstock.

"Not for a couple of days. We need to get a ballistics guy in there, and given the number of bullets… Is there somewhere safe you can go?"

"I'll figure something out. Could I get my purse and briefcase, at least? I left them both near the front door."

"I'll see what we can do."

Raleigh followed Abe Comstock out of the office and into the marble-tiled lobby and found Griffin waiting for her. Someone had loaned him a shirt, a bit snug across his broad shoulders, but at least it wasn't stained with blood. She wanted more than anything to return to the solace of his warm embrace. But what might have been appropriate in the midst of an emergency didn't seem so now.

"How about we go to the hospital?" Raleigh asked.

Griffin frowned. "Not necessary."

She shook her head. The big strong man didn't want to show weakness. "Maybe you need a transfusion. Antibiotics."

He shook his head. "I'm good. Stop worrying."

His color was better, at least. And he was no longer wobbling like a colt trying to find its legs.

"What now?"

That question was answered when Jillian Baxter, Daniel's ever-efficient personal assistant, waltzed into the lobby as if she owned the place. She had a knack for getting past guards and doormen. All she had to do was show them Daniel's business card.

Jillian looked stylish and polished as always, her chin-length blond bob sleek and her skinny black jeans and gauzy striped shirt screaming classy-casual.

"Looks like you two have gotten yourselves into a sticky wicket." Her voice held just the hint of an English accent. "I've got the limo outside. Daniel insists you both stay at his home for as long as necessary. The dog, too, of course."

Griffin and Raleigh exchanged a look. "Did you call him?" he asked.

She shook her head. "Daniel has ways of finding out everything. He might have been listening to the police scanner."

"Or," Jillian said with a smile, "the building manager might have called him."

"Oh, right." Raleigh turned to Griffin. "Daniel owns this building."

Ha. He'd known there was more to the story of why Raleigh chose to live here. Daniel apparently offered secure and convenient living spaces for his employees. Nice perk.

Griffin found the invitation to stay at Daniel's home undeniably tempting. For one night, at least, he wouldn't have to worry about Raleigh's safety and he could get some sleep. He'd heard Daniel Logan's River Oaks mansion was a veritable fortress with more security than the Pentagon.

"Maybe just for one night," Raleigh said, echoing his thoughts. "We can regroup in the morning. If we're lucky, the police will have caught the shooter."

Griffin didn't share her optimism. He was willing to bet their shooter hadn't left behind a single fingerprint or shell casing. He'd covered his tracks pretty well so far—his phone call untraceable, his voice disguised. His initial communications to Griffin had been through throwaway email addresses that led to dead ends.

"All right. One night." He wasn't in any shape to get work done tonight anyway. His brain was sluggish from whatever drugs he'd been crazy enough to consent to.

"Marvelous." Jillian produced a clipboard from her voluminous purse, reminiscent of Mary Poppins. "Griffin, given that you are a reporter, Daniel asks that you sign this before coming to his home. It's just to protect his privacy."

With a sigh, Griffin read the short document. It was a blanket off-the-record agreement, meaning he couldn't write about anything he saw or heard in Daniel's home. Normally Griffin wouldn't agree to such terms. But he had no choice, not if he wanted to stay with Raleigh.

And he did. It wasn't a matter of her safety anymore. They had both come close to dying tonight, and that meant they shared a bond no one else would understand. He simply did not want to be far from her right now.

He signed the form and handed the clipboard back to Jillian. "Your boss doesn't miss a beat, does he?"

"He's very thorough," Jillian said cheerfully. "The limo is waiting in the garage."

Griffin said nothing as he, Raleigh and Copper

were safe in the back of the limo and Randall had pulled out of the garage. But he felt guilty as hell. He'd assumed he could keep Raleigh safe on a short trip from her office to her home. He'd picked up on a few useful skills when he'd written for *Soldier of Fortune,* hanging out with mercenaries who were constantly on the watch for snipers and booby traps.

But had he missed something, some clue that would have told a formally trained bodyguard like Randall that something was amiss, and they shouldn't enter her apartment?

Griffin sat across from Raleigh, next to the fridge, which he opened. Bottled orange juice, that should help. They always gave him orange juice when he donated blood. "Want anything?" he asked as he uncapped his bottle.

"Not right now."

He checked to make sure the glass partition between front and back seats was up. "So, what did you tell the cops? I saw our buddy Abe Comstock hanging around." Griffin was dying to know what Raleigh had revealed. He had fudged a lot, hoping to protect his story, but it would look bad if he and Raleigh had contradicted each other.

"Comstock questioned me, but he was actually pretty civil. I think tonight might have convinced him I'm onto something."

"That's good, at least."

"I told him everything, Griffin. I'm sorry if that compromises your story."

"It might." He shrugged, as if he really didn't care very much.

"No other reporter was there," she reminded him. "No matter what some other reporter writes, your story will be better."

He held his juice bottle up in a mock toast. "Thanks for the vote of confidence."

Griffin observed her for a while as she stared out the window. She still looked troubled. He wished there was some way he could reassure her, but bland, soothing words wouldn't do the trick. Raleigh needed facts to convince her of anything, and facts about this situation were few and far between. He simply couldn't connect the dots.

"Griffin, I'm really sorry about how I acted."

Griffin struggled to figure out what she was referring to. And failed. Hadn't she already apologized earlier? "What?"

"When you were injured. I…I was so busy worrying about the cracked glass on a photograph that I didn't even notice you were dripping blood."

Really? He honestly hadn't been paying attention to her actions. He'd been pretty wrapped up with his own injury. "It was a confusing time. Everything happened fast."

"Then, once I saw you were injured, I was still

completely useless. I... I..." She swallowed, unable to continue.

"What are you talking about? You got me to the sofa. You brought me towels."

"Before that. It was the b-blood."

Griffin wanted to smack himself in the forehead as he recalled her tears. No wonder she'd been so upset. This wasn't the first time she'd been in an incident that involved a lot of blood. He sifted through what he'd read about the accident that had killed her husband.

"You did fine."

"I fell apart," she corrected him. "I had some kind of flashback or something. To the day Jason died. Up until tonight, I never remembered what happened. But seeing all that blood must have triggered something."

"Maybe you weren't strong enough to handle those memories before," Griffin said, wanting to offer some comfort.

"That's not the point. What if you'd died? And there I was, a puddle on the floor, not even noticing. I was somewhere in the past, worrying about events that can't be changed, instead of living in the present."

Hallelujah. He'd known that for a long time. Now wasn't the time to gloat, however. He capped his juice and stuck it in a cup holder, then swiveled from his seat to settle in next to her, sliding his good arm around her shoulders. "You are way too hard on yourself."

"Someone needs to be," she muttered.

"I don't think so. I think someone needs to pamper you and take care of you—"

"I can take care of—"

"For one evening, okay? I'm not saying you can't be independent and take care of yourself. But every once in a while, you need to let go. I admire that you are so passionate and dedicated to your work, and I even admire your loyalty to Jason. But there's more to life."

"Very profound. Since when did you become my therapist?" But she didn't put a lot of bite into the reprimand, possibly because she knew he was right. She had to know.

"You're wound up tighter than a coiled rattler."

"Because someone tried to kill me. I'm entitled."

"Just relax, would you? Lean back against me. Close your eyes."

Surprisingly, she followed his directions. "I don't like the pictures I see when I close my eyes," she confessed.

"Don't think about that. Listen to my voice. Drop your shoulders." She had them hunched almost to her ears.

Gradually, her shoulders relaxed. Even Copper, who had been standing on his hind legs looking excitedly out the window, settled into her lap.

"Drop your chin to your chest—slowly. No jerking. Now, rock your head slowly and gently from shoulder to shoulder."

She did as he said. "Hmm. This actually feels kind of good."

If he'd had two good arms, he would have rubbed her shoulders.

"When we get to Daniel's house, take a long, hot bath. Drink some wine." Just thinking about Raleigh, reclined in a steaming bubble bath, made Griffin go hard. As close as she was now, he could smell her shampoo, something lemony. Her hair was no longer slicked back in its usual sleek style. At some point during the evening her clip had come loose. Now the auburn strands had fallen into tousled disarray, a bit of natural curl asserting itself.

He'd bet she hadn't thought to look in a mirror lately. She would probably be horrified. But he liked the look.

She leaned her head against his shoulder. "This is nice."

"Yes, it is."

"I wish the limo ride was longer. It's so quiet in here. Can't even hear the traffic noises."

"We could ask Randall to go around the block a few times."

"Tempting. But Daniel will be impatient to see us and find out what happened firsthand."

Duty again.

What would it take to get Raleigh to relax and put herself first?

## CHAPTER TEN

Soon enough, the limo pulled up to an ornate, wrought-iron gate, which opened noiselessly. The limo glided through, then down a long driveway to a four—no, five-car—garage attached to the biggest private residence Griffin had ever seen, if he didn't count the royal palace in Saudi Arabia.

The house was built of brown bricks that appeared worn by centuries of weather, like an abbey in the English countryside.

"No houses in Houston are very old," he said. "Why does this place look…aged?"

"Daniel's father had the bricks imported from Scotland. They were from a cathedral that was torn down."

With the ivy-covered walls, mullioned windows and mature live oak trees, the house made quite an impression.

When the driver opened their door, Jillian was already standing outside the limo, waiting for them. "Sorry to bring you in the back way your first visit."

"I've been here before," Raleigh said as the driver

offered his hand to help her out of the car. "For my job interview."

"Oh, of course, I remember."

Randall offered a hand to Griffin, too. He wasn't in that bad a shape, was he? He climbed out under his own power with a nod of thanks to Randall for the offer of help.

"The front entrance is quite impressive, though," Raleigh said. "We'll have to show Griffin later."

*Why? I can't write a word about it.* Nor could he write anything about tonight's incident. The story was too incomplete for *Currents.* And if he fed the information piecemeal to the newspaper—

Hell, he should resign from the *Telegram.* It wasn't fair to accept a salary when he was holding out. He should bank on getting the TV job. It was a risk, but he wasn't averse to risk, as his life up to this point proved.

"We'll go in through the kitchen," Jillian said. "If I'm not mistaken, Daniel will have dinner ready."

She wasn't mistaken. The smell hit him the moment he walked inside the house—roasting meat, garlic and onions and spices that immediately made his mouth water and his stomach rumble. Now that the adrenaline rush had leaked away, he realized he was starving.

The limo driver disappeared, and Jillian led them down a long, tiled hallway into a kitchen the size of

a gymnasium, where a chef in a uniform and a puffy
hat worked over an indoor grill.

A chef. Daniel had a real chef, employed in his
kitchen for every day. This kind of wealth was mind-
boggling, and Griffin was once again irritated that
he couldn't write about it. The whole world would
be interested in how Daniel Logan lived. He was a
minor celebrity, this son of an oil billionaire who
had spent six years in the penitentiary for a murder
he hadn't committed. His reclusive nature made him
that much more intriguing.

"What is that animal doing in my kitchen?" the
obviously French chef wanted to know. He stared
down his nose at Raleigh and Copper.

"Just passing through," Jillian said breezily. "Come
this way, please."

They ventured from the kitchen and into a great
room with a vaulted ceiling, stone fireplace and several seating areas. At one end of the room was a
carved mahogany bar, behind which Daniel himself
stood, uncorking a bottle of red wine.

Copper leaped from Raleigh's arms and ran toward
the fireplace as fiercely as a five-pound dog could at
a golden retriever, stretched out near the hearth as if
there were a fire burning.

"Copper," Raleigh said, "mind your manners."

The big dog raised his head, then seemed to smile

and wagged his tail enthusiastically as he lumbered to his feet. Copper went still as the retriever sniffed him.

"Tucker," Daniel said to the dog, "be a good host and show your guest where the doggy door is. And share your dinner."

The dog looked questioningly at his master.

"Go on, outside."

Tucker was quick to obey, and Copper trotted at the bigger dog's heels with a happy yip, having suddenly found a new friend.

"Are you sure…?" Raleigh looked worriedly after the dogs.

"They'll be fine. Tucker is big, but he wouldn't hurt a flea." Daniel abandoned his task and came around to embrace Raleigh. "I am so glad you're okay, Raleigh. When I heard what happened, I felt terrible. I've always prided myself on how safe that building is. Now I find out it's not. I'm thinking of replacing all the windows with bulletproof glass."

Griffin couldn't imagine how much that would cost, but it was probably pocket change for Daniel.

"That's thoughtful of you, Daniel," Raleigh said. "But it's certainly not your fault. Someone had to work pretty hard to get to me. The police said the bullets came from the building across the street, one of the upper stories—not from the street."

"Yes, I've already talked to Lieutenant Comstock."

Of course he had. This guy appeared to have access to everybody.

"Griffin. It's wonderful to meet you in person." He shook Griffin's hand with a firm grip, looking him straight in the eye in a way that made Griffin feel oddly special. Daniel had charisma oozing from his pores. "I want to personally thank you for seeing to Raleigh's safety. You saved her life."

"It was a wild bullet," Griffin said, knowing that it was pure chance that he got hit instead of Raleigh. "This…this stalker is pretty desperate."

"We'll find out who it is. The police are taking the case very seriously. Have you told them about the other matters? The rogue deposit and the falsified phone bill? The threatening phone call?"

"I told them everything," Raleigh said. "As much as I could remember. I was pretty rattled."

"Understandably. We'll see what they do with the information. Part of me is relieved they're on the case. Another part of me wishes the police would just stay out of it." He cast a worried glance at Griffin. "I understand this cramps your, um, journalistic endeavors."

The man understood more than Griffin would have guessed. "We have to put Raleigh's safety first," Griffin said. He was in a quandary about what to write, and when. He felt his loyalties had gone into a blender.

"Where are my manners? Please, sit down and let me pour you a glass of wine. Or maybe you'd prefer beer? I have some excellent examples from various Texas microbreweries."

Griffin would have been happy with a plain ol' Bud right about now. "I would love a beer. You can pick something for me."

"That merlot you were uncorking looks fabulous," Raleigh said as she sank onto a buff-colored leather sofa.

"Jillian? Will you stay and have dinner with us?"

"Thank you, Daniel. But if you don't need me, I believe I'll retire early."

"I'll have a plate sent to your quarters, then."

Jillian smiled. "That's thoughtful, thank you. Good night." She addressed Griffin and Raleigh. "If you need anything, there's a phone in every room with a Jillian button."

Griffin was sure he recognized a spark of yearning in her gray eyes whenever Jillian looked at her boss. It would take a strong woman not to fall for a good-looking, rich and seemingly generous and concerned guy like Daniel, especially if she lived and worked with him on a constant basis.

"She's good," Raleigh said. "You need to give that girl a raise."

Daniel smiled. "She's a gem, all right. Well paid, trust me."

Griffin saw no answering spark in Daniel. He spoke of Jillian with fondness, nothing more. Poor Jillian.

And why did Griffin even care? He fumed again over the fact that he couldn't write about any of it. He'd never felt so frustrated in his life.

A server brought in a tray of appetizers—Brie cheese, crackers and tart apple slices. How many employees did this guy support single-handedly? Griffin saw only the tip of the iceberg, he was sure.

A few minutes later, the server, Manuel, announced that dinner was ready. They all filed into a formal dining room and sat at a round table graced with fine linens, crystal and sterling silver flatware.

Is this how Daniel ate dinner every night? As if in a four-star restaurant?

The dinner was certainly one of the best Griffin had ever eaten, including a selection of grilled meats, a baked artichoke-heart casserole, tender asparagus, some kind of whole-grain rolls that melted in his mouth.

Fresh fruit and rich vanilla ice cream for dessert.

All of it was accompanied by free-flowing wine, beer and port with dark chocolate to top everything off. Egads.

Daniel was a skilled conversationalist, steering

the discussion away from the evening's disturbing events, drawing each of them out in turn, adding an amusing anecdote of his own when appropriate.

He apparently hadn't always been a recluse. Before his incarceration, it sounded as though he'd led a normal, if privileged, life. He'd gone to Princeton, pledged a fraternity, played sports.

"I'm sure you both must be tired," Daniel finally said as Manuel began clearing the table. "Since I let Jillian go for the night, I'll show you to your rooms. There's a media room in your wing with all kinds of amusements if you'd like to stay up awhile. There's a kitchenette with snacks, too. I hope you'll make yourselves at home. Both of you can stay here as long as necessary."

"I have work to do," Raleigh objected. "I have to be at the office early tomorrow."

"Nonsense. You're taking a vacation, Raleigh, starting now. You haven't had any time off in years. Garrett can make court appearances and file papers for you."

"Garrett? He's barely out of law school."

"Smart and extremely capable, or I wouldn't have hired him. I'll set up a meeting with him tomorrow morning."

"I...okay," she said meekly. It was hard to argue with such a forceful personality.

Good. If Daniel ordered Raleigh to stay here, Griffin could go about his business without worrying about her safety. And maybe he could finally get to the bottom of this mess.

They took an elevator—an elevator!—to the third floor, which housed a guest wing. Raleigh was assigned to a room with blue silk-covered walls and elaborately carved walnut furnishings. Real Persian rugs. Fancier than the fanciest hotel Griffin had ever seen, that was for sure.

"Thank you, Daniel. I'll see you both in the morning." She closed her door firmly, but she couldn't close the door on Griffin's fantasies. Already he was picturing her in that bed, surrounded by silk bed linens and pillows, naked and willing in his arms.

He stifled a groan. This was no good.

"You have a thing for Raleigh," Daniel said as they continued down the hall. A statement, not a question.

No use denying it. Daniel was no idiot. "She's an incredible woman. Smart, beautiful, and completely unattainable."

"She's had a hard go of it. But it's time for her to move on."

"I couldn't agree more. But it probably won't be with me."

"Why do you say that? You're single, unattached."

"And firmly committed to staying that way. I'm never at home. The closest I came to a lasting relationship was when I bought a cactus. Died after three months."

"That's too bad. I think the two of you might make a nice match."

"Temporarily, maybe. Which is exactly why I'm not pushing it."

"I appreciate your integrity. Because if you hurt her, I'd have to string you up by your, um, big toes."

He could, too. With enough money, you could ruin anyone's life. Look how easily someone had derailed Raleigh's.

"I'll keep that in mind."

Griffin's room was more masculine but no less luxurious than Raleigh's. The private bathroom was an exercise in self-indulgence with granite walls that shone like mirrors. The walk-in shower alone was bigger than his bedroom at home.

Nothing had been left to chance. Griffin found two changes of clothes—his size and even his taste—and all the toiletries he could possibly need. Daniel, or maybe Jillian, was a freaking mind reader.

He indulged in the shower, trying not to get his bandage too wet, then wrapped himself in a feather-soft terry robe he found hanging on the back of the door.

It was only ten o'clock, and though he was short on sleep, he knew he was too restless to lie down. He wandered down to the end of the hall, where the media room was located, hoping to find a diversion there.

What he found was Raleigh, sitting in a huge, cushy chair with a book and a glass of wine. She didn't hear him come in, so for a few seconds he had the pleasure of studying her.

She was wrapped in a robe, but nothing like his bulky terry garment. Hers was blue silk that exactly matched the walls in her room, and it draped over her slender body, showing a surprising amount of curves and displaying the subtle valley between her breasts at the neckline.

She had one leg tucked under her, but the other was bare from mid-thigh down, peeking out from the opening of the robe. She had beautiful, slender ankles and her toenails were painted a delicate pink. That little hint of femininity pleased him. It told him she hadn't forgotten she was a woman, even if she chose to hide that side of herself most of the time.

She'd washed her hair and it was still damp, drying in a muss of waves. He remembered the lush curls he'd seen in the old photos of her and Jason.

Though he hadn't made any noise, Raleigh looked up suddenly. "Oh. I didn't expect anyone else to be up."

"Couldn't sleep," he said as he walked all the way into the room and sat down on a love seat near Raleigh's chair. "Too many thoughts chasing their tails through my head."

"Me, too. I found this book on the shelf about quantum physics. I thought it would bore me into a coma, but no such luck. It's fascinating."

"At least it's taking your mind off your…troubling thoughts."

"Yeah. For a while, anyway." She put the book aside without marking her place and adjusted the robe so it covered more of her chest. "I wish Daniel had provided me with a robe like yours, instead of this flimsy thing." Then she touched her hair self-consciously. "I'm not really put together well right now."

"I think you look fantastic," Griffin couldn't help saying. "Blue is a good color for you. And your hair looks…sexy."

"Why do you have to say things like that?"

"Because they're true."

"You make me uncomfortable, you know."

"It's not my intention. Well, maybe it is, a little," he said with a grin. "I want so badly to hold you. But those stone walls around your heart are a mile high and three feet thick."

"I'm guessing it's not my heart you're after."

He thought about that for a few moments. What did he want? More than what he usually wanted from a woman, despite what he'd just told Daniel. He'd seldom felt such a strong need for any woman's company, in or out of bed. In unguarded moments, he fantasized not just about sex with Raleigh, but about sharing small, sweet moments with her. Holding her hand. Watching a sunset.

It was crazy.

"I want more than a quick roll in the hay."

She looked a little surprised by his admission. "You know, maybe that's why I'm so scared of you. If all you wanted was sex, it wouldn't be quite so threatening. I have...needs, after all."

"So if I was some sleazeball player who wanted to screw you, then never see your face again, you might be tempted?"

She folded her arms protectively across her chest. "You don't have to put it that way."

"It's immaterial, because I don't want you that way. You're worth more than a quick lay."

"Thank you. I think."

"I'm not looking for gratitude. Look, Raleigh, there's something between us, and it's not one-sided. I see it in your eyes, I feel it rolling off you in waves. Why are you fighting it? We're two single adults who like each other and have a strong, mutual physical attraction."

"I don't think of myself as single," she said on a sigh. "I'm a widow. You don't love someone the way I loved Jason, then just toss it away."

"I'm not asking you to forget the man. But you might consider putting things in perspective. It's been six years."

"It might be another six before I'm ready. I might

never be ready. My grief counselor said everyone heals at their own pace."

Griffin wished he could get five minutes alone in a dark alley with that grief counselor.

"I'm sorry," she said a little desperately.

This was not working. He had to get away from her and get his head back where it belonged, with his story. If he couldn't sleep, he could work on the story, prepare for the day when he would have all he needed to send to CNI and get the green light.

"Okay." He slapped his hands against his knees in a gesture of finality, then stood and headed to a bookcase, where he saw a laptop computer. Daniel wouldn't mind if he borrowed it for the evening. He grabbed the computer and headed for the door. "I'll see you in the morning."

He was about to close the door when a single word froze him in place. "Wait."

He turned and looked at her.

"I came in here because I just couldn't lie in bed, alone. I remembered the accident today. Now I understand why I suppressed it."

"Bad, huh?"

"The kind of bad I wouldn't wish on anyone." She shuddered slightly. "When I was a kid, I had nightmares about this big, black bull chasing me. But I was afraid to tell anyone about it. Night after night I would lie in bed and try not to close my eyes. But I always did."

"It doesn't surprise me, that you didn't tell anyone. You were probably determined to be self-sufficient even then."

She smiled, a little sadly. "I guess I was."

"Would it—" He stopped and thought very hard about what he said next, because he wanted to be very sure he meant it. He examined his conscience for ulterior motives and, honestly, couldn't find any. "Would it help if I held you? Because I could do that. With no thought or expectation of anything more. I could hold you until you fell asleep."

She started to shake her head, an immediate, reflexive action.

"Uh-uh, think about it first," he said.

"I couldn't ask you."

"You're not asking. I'm offering. I'm insisting." He put the computer aside and went to her. "Either of us could easily have died today. I don't want to be alone, either. We can wear all our clothes. No funny business."

Slowly, she nodded. "I think I would like that. Two...friends, keeping the monsters at bay."

"Exactly." It would be physical torture to have her so close, in bed, and not do anything about it. But if he could do something to take some of her pain away, to make her feel safer, he was willing. "Your room or mine?"

"Mine, I think."

He walked slowly toward her and offered his hand. "Come on, then."

It seemed to take forever, but she finally reached up and took his hand. They walked down the hallway together, holding hands like two old friends.

## CHAPTER ELEVEN

WHAT HAD SHE been thinking?

Oh, sure, snuggle up to big, strong, almost naked, great-smelling single guy who you *know* has the hots for you. In a bed made up with vanilla-scented silk sheets. And *nothing will happen.*

She'd wanted a simple distraction from her disturbing thoughts. Sooner or later she would have to absorb those memories of the accident. Absorb them, process them, put them in perspective—all those things mentally healthy people did so they could function normally.

But she wasn't ready for that, and it had seemed like a good idea at the time to accept the offer of a strong shoulder to lean against, someone she wouldn't have to do a lot of explaining to.

Now here she was, in bed with Griffin. He wore a pair of boxer shorts and a T-shirt, which she suspected was a concession to her. He probably slept in the nude. And she was still in her robe and nightgown, though both were so thin they offered little protection.

To his credit, he'd been a complete gentleman. He

had put his arm around her, let her cuddle up next to him like a puppy, turned out the light, and hadn't said or done anything since, and that had been ten or fifteen minutes ago.

He wasn't asleep, though. His breathing hadn't gone slow, deep and regular, and he wasn't quite relaxed enough to be sleeping.

"Are you comfortable?" he whispered.

"Yes. Are you?"

"I'm fine."

She was comfortable and not the least bit sleepy. Instead, she was plenty distracted. Griffin's plan had worked a little too well. She tried to summon a memory of Jason—her husband, alive and well, laughing, teasing her. But the picture that came to mind was thready, insubstantial, like an old home movie that had been run too many times through the projector.

How much easier it was to picture Griffin. The memories were so fresh, the images so vibrant she could almost…no, she *was* touching him. Her hand rested on his chest, and she could feel his heart beating slow and steady. Up her arm and all the way through her body, she could feel his heart…

She was afraid to move. Afraid of what her body might do totally independent from her will.

"You're tense," Griffin said.

"I know."

"You can change your mind. I'll slink off to my own bedroom."

He was giving her an out. The sane thing was to take it. "No, please stay. Maybe if you...remember how you talked to me in the limo? You helped me relax then."

"I can do that. Start with your breathing. In to the count of five, out to the count of five. Fill your belly with oxygen."

She did as he said, completely trusting him. After a minute of so of deep breathing, she could feel herself relaxing.

"How do you know this stuff?" she asked.

"Shh. We're going to do progressive muscle relaxing. Start with your scalp. Feel your scalp and how it covers your skull. Now let every tiny muscle in your scalp relax..."

He progressed to her face, her jaw, her neck, her shoulders. She didn't remember much past her chest and lungs, because she fell asleep.

When next she was aware, sunlight streamed through her curtains and a warm, male body lay beneath her. Jason—no. Her head was tucked beneath his chin, and she inhaled deeply of his skin and knew it wasn't Jason.

She suffered a moment or two of confusion, and then she remembered. Griffin. He'd spent the whole night in her bed, and now she had her arms and legs wrapped around him. He had one hand on her bottom and the other on her breast, and his deep, gentle breathing told her he was asleep.

She certainly wasn't, not anymore. Her body tingled with awareness and her mind filled with erotic images of her and Griffin—more vivid than they'd been before.

Suddenly the effort of denying what her body wanted was just too much work. Her brain went on strike, simply refusing to tell her how to extricate herself from this sticky situation of her own making.

Maybe consciously she hadn't intended this to happen, but on some level, she'd been hoping to ease herself into an intimate situation with Griffin. She hadn't made any monumental decision to abandon her six-plus years of celibacy; rather, the day's events had organically led to her and Griffin in bed, their hands all over each other's bodies.

His T-shirt rode up, revealing a strip of his tanned abs. Knowing it was dangerous, Raleigh moved her hand down until her fingers flirted with his bare skin. So warm. So vibrant. So alive.

She shoved the bedcovers back and her breath caught in her throat. She had a clear view of Griffin's erection. She knew men often had erections in the morning. She'd been married, after all. But she couldn't help feeling that this one was for her. He was cupping her breast.

He wouldn't object if she changed her mind. Griffin had made it pretty clear he would welcome sex with her. If they crossed that line, it would be just sex and friendship, she reminded herself. He hadn't alluded to anything more.

He wanted her, she wanted him, pure and simple. No exchange of heavy emotions need be involved.

Raleigh turned her head and pressed her lips into his neck, touching just the tip of her tongue to his skin, tasting him.

"Raleigh?"

The low rumble of his sleep-roughened voice startled her. "Um…good morning."

"I'll say." He made no effort to move his hands. "What's going through your mind? And you better tell me fast. Because in about ten seconds, words won't be necessary. Or welcome."

"Words are overrated." Who needed explanations? It was pretty clear what was going on here.

She pressed her hand against his chest, raising up so she could kiss him on the mouth. What was left of her brain melted on contact. It was the most inviting, sexiest, warmest kiss on earth.

With a groan, Griffin rolled her onto her back, bracing her head on either side with his big, capable hands and kissing her with an intensity and a thoroughness that took her breath away. She squirmed with the need to feel him all over her, inside her. Her private parts tingled like a limb that had gone to sleep and was just now waking up. The sensation was so pleasurable, yet almost painful at the same time.

Her silk robe's belt was already loose. Griffin worked one hand inside the robe, then found her bare thigh. Her nightgown had already worked itself up around her hips, and she wasn't wearing panties.

"Raleigh. Oh, my—you have the sexiest ass I've ever seen on any woman. And your belly. I have to see." He raked the gown up higher, revealing everything to his hungry gaze. He got up on his knees so he could lean down and kiss her belly, working his warm kisses lower, stroking her thighs, teasing her legs open.

"Do you—" Her brain was having trouble forming words, but she wasn't so far gone she'd forgotten one important thing. "We need—"

The kisses slowed, then stopped. "You think I carry it around in my wallet?"

She couldn't help laughing, on the edge of hysteria at the thought that they might not be able to consummate their mutual and rather frightening lust. "I've heard that's not a good thing to do. Your body heat—"

He groaned. "I'm gonna die here and now."

"The bathroom. It's incredibly well stocked. Disposable razors, feminine products—"

"Don't move. I mean it. Don't move and don't think too hard."

She wouldn't. She would stay in suspended animation until he came back. Seconds later, she heard a victorious "Yesss!" and she nearly wept. Bless

Daniel. Or Jillian. Or whoever the gods of illicit sex were.

When Griffin returned to bed, he was gloriously naked. She quickly followed suit, though the only thing still actually on her body was the silly wisp of a silky nightgown she'd found in the room, like nothing she would ever buy for herself. She whisked it over her head, letting it float to the floor in a blue-gossamer cloud.

She could see that Griffin approved. His eyes darkened, and he opened his mouth slightly, taking in more air.

Letting her instincts guide her, she held her arms open. It seemed so wanton, all this naked flesh in the bright, cheery sunshine. Sex like this was more suitable for the dark. But she was glad for the light, because she wanted to experience this coming together with all of her senses, including sight.

Griffin was a beautiful example of the male species.

He rejoined her on the bed, drawing her against him, kissing her again until she was dizzy with longing to be one with him. He coaxed her legs open again, stroking her folds with boldly curious fingers. She was as hot and slick as she'd ever been, her flesh aching to have him inside her.

"Oh, Griffin. Do it, please. I can't wait any longer. I'm going to burn up."

"Whatever you want, honey." He pulled away from

her only long enough to sheathe himself. Then he covered her body with his, settling into the cradle of her thighs, letting her get used to his weight.

He probed her entrance with his erection and she took a deep breath. It had been such a long time. She was a virgin all over again, at least that's what it felt like.

He pushed inside. "You're tight."

"It's good." She didn't want him worrying about hurting her. He pushed deeper, stretching her just to the bounds of comfort. But there was no pain, just a delicious fullness, and she lifted her hips and thrust upward to meet him. She wanted all of him, all that he would give her, and he obliged, thrusting himself to the hilt.

She gasped just as he did—with pleasure, with the surprise of how incredibly good it actually felt. It went beyond mere physical satisfaction. He completed her, filled her from head to toe with a deep sense of satisfaction.

She basked in the warmth of their union as he pushed in and pulled out, slowly at first, building to a delicious cadence like a well-crafted symphony. He filled her physically, but on some other level, too. She surrendered to him until she couldn't bear one more moment. Yet she held back, wanting it to last forever.

Finally she toppled over the edge, putting a fist in her mouth to stifle the scream she longed for. They were somewhat isolated in the guest wing of Daniel's house, but if she let it out, she was pretty sure everyone within several blocks would hear her.

"Good, Raleigh, so good. You're so beautiful, incredible, I've never…" She let his praises settle around her like flower petals. Yes, it was good, and it was even better when she watched his facial muscles tighten as he struggled for control, then lost the battle and unleashed himself inside her, burying his face in the pillow beside her head to muffle his own cries of ecstasy.

Griffin collapsed, panting as if he'd just sprinted across a football field.

"Raleigh."

"Mmm." She was less articulate than him, even.

She reveled in the tingly afterglow for as long as she dared. They barely moved, except when Griffin shifted his weight off her. She never wanted it to end, as all good things inevitably did.

"Honey?"

"Yes?"

"I'll probably kick myself for asking, but I'm naturally curious. What changed your mind?"

"I didn't really change my mind," she admitted. "It's just that my body went off and did its own thing and my mind took a vacation."

"Ah."

"No regrets, though." He didn't deserve that. He'd given of himself from his very depths, and she had to be grateful—no, awed—by the generous nature of his lovemaking. "Thank you."

He laughed. "You gotta be kidding."

"I'm not. You were there for me, when I needed you."

"I'll always—" He stopped, cleared his throat.

He'd been about to say he'd always be there for her. An automatic rejoinder, and he'd thought better of it, she was sure. At least he was honest. "I'm glad I helped you through what could have been a tough night."

Her thanks extended way past last night. But she supposed a postmortem of everyone's motivations wasn't necessary. This wasn't a case to take to court.

She glanced at her watch. "It's late. I have to meet with Garrett this morning." She sighed. "I'd like to stay here awhile longer. But the real world is knocking."

"The real world can be a bitch sometimes." He kissed her on the nose, then released her from his embrace so she could slip out of bed. She was suddenly cold as she walked naked to the bathroom.

GRIFFIN SLUMPED back against the pillows as Raleigh closed the bathroom door on the enticing sight of her bare bottom.

Damn. That had been as pleasurable as it had been unexpected. His body was satiated in a way that was new to him, yet he already wondered how and when he could have her again.

For those few insane minutes when they'd made love, she'd been completely open to him, unguarded. For the first time, he thought he'd seen the real Raleigh.

He'd liked it. As he'd stared into those guileless green eyes, so trusting, he'd felt something blooming in his chest besides desire. Something that felt a lot like love, or at least the potential for love.

That was new. Most of his relationships had involved him trying not to say or do anything that implied commitment. A couple of times he hadn't been clear enough, and he'd ended up breaking some poor girl's heart and feeling like a heel.

With Raleigh, he'd almost told her he would always be there for her—and meant it. He'd censored himself, though, not because he feared being misunderstood, but because he wasn't quite ready for her to see what was in his heart.

Thank God he'd stopped himself. He was in no position to make promises. He'd chosen a lifestyle that didn't accommodate happily ever after.

He had to get his head back on straight. His work had always been his top priority. That hadn't changed just because one beautiful, intriguing, vulnerable woman had let him past her defenses. Once.

He heard the shower running and decided it would be better if he was gone when she finished bathing.

If not, if he saw her all rosy-pink from the warm water, smelling of whatever fancy shampoo Daniel undoubtedly provided, he might be tempted to bundle Raleigh right back into bed.

Griffin quickly pulled on his boxers and T-shirt, though probably no one would be roaming the halls. As far as he could tell, he and Raleigh were alone in the guest wing.

He paused on his way out the door. Raleigh's briefcase sat open on a small, antique writing desk, and sunlight glinted off something inside, drawing his eye.

Taking a couple of steps closer, he saw that it was a small, framed photo of Jason.

They had escaped her apartment with little more than the dog and the clothes on their backs, yet Raleigh managed to have a picture of her dead husband with her. She probably kept it in her briefcase, and when she'd arrived here, the first thing she had done was open the case and look at that picture.

Damn. Disappointment pressed against him from every direction. He had thought maybe Raleigh had made a breakthrough. But it was clear who took precedence in her life. Yeah, she'd made love with *him* this morning, not Jason. But only because Jason wasn't available.

He should have questioned her more closely. Her change of heart, the fact that she had initiated sex when last night she'd been firmly against it, should have tipped him off that something wasn't right.

Now he understood what she'd meant about her body making the decision, rather than her brain. Nothing had changed. And unless he wanted to play second fiddle to the sainted Jason, he needed to make sure this did not happen again. He didn't particularly like the feeling of being Jason's surrogate.

He should have been able to simply shrug and walk away. But it was time for him to admit that what he felt for Raleigh was more than lust, more than mere affection. She had become a priority in his life, and protecting her was more important than anything else—including his story.

Including his career.

His dedication to finding out who wanted to hurt her wouldn't change. He *would* find out, and stop them. But he would no longer press Raleigh for more than she could give.

RALEIGH COULDN'T REMEMBER the last time she'd felt this light. As she let the warm water cascade down her body, she relived Griffin's hands roaming at will, seeking and getting responses from her like a virtuoso playing a violin.

It was as if every emotion from the past several years had been bottled up inside, and Griffin had pulled the cork. She wanted to laugh and cry at the same time, to dance and hit something. She wanted to hug her dog.

She was starving. She hoped Daniel stayed true to form and fed them a huge, greasy breakfast. Her usual fruit and yogurt did not sound appealing in the least.

Daniel had provided every cosmetic or toiletry she could possibly wish for, including a mango/grapefruit body lotion that smelled fantastic. She slathered it over every inch of her skin, brushed and flossed and dabbed on a bit of makeup.

She plugged in the blow dryer, then straightened her hair as she always did.

Her hair didn't really matter that much, did it? The only person she would be meeting with was Garrett. But somehow, the habitual act of taming her mop helped her to feel more in control. She clipped it back into a ponytail and smoothed back any strays from her face.

She had no idea what sort of clothing she would find in the closet, but she felt pretty sure it would fit. Daniel—or perhaps Jillian—had a magic touch when it came to anticipating guests' needs. She still couldn't believe Griffin had found condoms.

She opened the bathroom door. "Shower's all your—" The room was empty. Griffin was gone.

Sinking onto the rumpled bed, Raleigh tried to tamp down her disappointment. What had she expected? That he would stick to her side 24/7? He'd probably wanted his own shower, his own things. In fact, yes, she could hear his shower going.

In the closet she found a variety of casual clothes. Nothing like she usually wore for work, but she was officially on vacation according to Daniel. She chose a pair of stone-washed jeans and was amazed at how well they fit and how comfortable they were. Her closet at home held a couple of pairs of old jeans, but she seldom wore them.

She made a note of the size and brand, intending to purchase a pair for herself. She went to her briefcase to find the notebook she knew was there, and stopped cold when she saw Jason's picture, smiling up at her in that frozen, timeless way. "Oh, Jason." She picked up the picture and touched the glass over his face. "Are you terribly disappointed in me?"

She felt sure he would have been okay if she'd started seeing someone. He'd been a generous man in life; no reason to think he would be stingy and possessive with her after his death.

But she didn't know what he would think about hot, frantic sex with a man she wasn't even dating.

"It was a little much, I guess. I underestimated how much I'd be tempted." She sighed and tucked Jason under some books, wondering if Griffin had seen the picture and, if so, what he'd made of it.

Minutes later, with her cell phone stuck in her pocket, she headed downstairs. Copper greeted her effusively, and Raleigh picked him up and held him close. "Are you having a good time visiting your uncle Daniel?" she asked as the dog licked her on the chin.

"I heard that." Daniel appeared in the doorway of the formal dining room. "I am not your dog's uncle."

"Good morning, Daniel."

"We're having breakfast on the patio today. It's a beautiful morning."

"Wonderful." She set Copper down, and the dog ran off, probably to find his new playmate, Tucker. The two dogs, though comically mismatched in size, seemed to get along famously.

"The police didn't find any sign of the shooter," Daniel said. "Just an open window in a vacant office across the street. No bullet casings, no hair or fiber, no witnesses."

"That's bad." Actually, she'd expected as much. Whoever was out to get her was very good at not getting caught.

"Where's Griffin?" Daniel asked.

Raleigh stepped carefully, worried that anything she said regarding Griffin would give her away. "I heard a shower running down the hall from me a while ago. I'm sure he'll be down shortly."

Breakfast was exactly what Raleigh was craving— fried eggs, pork sausage, toast slathered in butter, orange juice and strong coffee.

"We have all kinds of cereal, oatmeal, granola,

fresh fruit—would you prefer something like that?" Daniel asked as Raleigh took her seat at the large glass-topped table, shaded by the biggest umbrella she'd ever seen.

"Oh, no, this is fine."

"Really? I remember that you were kind of a health nut."

She didn't think of herself that way. "Usually I'm—sensible when it comes to my diet. But hey, I'm on vacation, right? Besides, something about almost dying has made me crave cholesterol."

Daniel smiled. "Plenty of that here." On his own plate, though, she noticed he had fresh melon, a whole-wheat muffin and a dish of plain yogurt. She supposed he couldn't eat the greasy stuff every day, even if his cook was happy to put it in front of him.

Jillian joined them, looking daisy fresh in a polka-dot sundress, a teeny black cardigan and black sandals. Daniel apparently didn't require a dress-for-success wardrobe from her so long as she did her job.

"Good morning, Raleigh. I hope you slept well."

"Very well, thank you." In part because of her warm, muscular pillow. Her heart sank a bit as she thought about Griffin. When she saw him again, she had to be prepared for however he chose to play it. She hoped he didn't give them away, not yet. She still hadn't come to terms with what she'd done—what they'd done. She wasn't ready for anyone else to know about it.

## CHAPTER TWELVE

RALEIGH HAD just taken her first bite of the spicy sausage when Griffin appeared looking mouthwatering in a striped golf shirt, a pair of khakis riding low on his lean hips—and the inevitable cowboy boots. The bandage around his arm was smaller than before. He must have taken care of that himself. Too bad—she would have been happy to help him apply a fresh bandage to that gorgeous bicep. His hair was still damp from his shower, his face shaved smooth.

"Morning." He chose a chair next to Jillian, rather than near Raleigh. When their eyes met, he quickly looked away.

What the hell was that about? Did he have regrets? He was the one who'd been pushing for something more, and she was the one who was supposed to feel guilty and remorseful.

She didn't feel guilty. More...worried. About the future. About whether she'd made a mistake, and would lose Griffin altogether, even as a friend.

Not even a smile for her?

Daniel filled Griffin in on the police investigation into the shooting.

Griffin took a few notes.

Conversation at the breakfast table veered toward lighter topics after that. Daniel and Jillian talked about his schedule for the day. Daniel and Griffin discussed college football—for need of a topic of discussion, rather than any real interest from either of them.

Raleigh mostly said nothing. The nourishing but heavy food she'd craved only a few minutes ago now sat leaden in her stomach. She had no idea how to act toward a man she'd just had wild, unexpected sex with.

After a few more minutes, Griffin wiped his mouth with his napkin and pushed his chair away from the table. "I'll need a ride to my car," he announced. "Can you provide one, Daniel? Or I can call a cab."

"I'll have Randall take you wherever you need to go, of course. But are you sure you want to leave?"

"The shooter is after Raleigh, not me. I have a job, and no one is giving me paid vacation. Plus, I have some leads to follow."

Raleigh was crushed. He was leaving? But she absolutely would not behave like some clinging vine. Just because they'd had sex didn't mean she had a claim to him. She did, however, want a minute alone with him, if she could manage it without making it a big deal.

"You'll be careful, won't you?" she couldn't help asking.

"As careful as I know how to be."

"Why don't I loan you a car," Daniel said. "One our homicidal friend won't recognize."

"He can take mine," Jillian said. "I don't need to be anywhere today."

"That's very generous—both of you."

Raleigh was relieved that Griffin was taking at least some precautions. Then something he'd said a few moments earlier hit her. "Leads? You didn't say anything about leads."

"I'll let you know if anything pans out."

He was holding out on her. But he was under no obligation to share everything with them. She felt sure he would speak up when it was appropriate.

Raleigh managed to loiter near the kitchen as Jillian handed over the keys to her Range Rover. "Third gear sticks a bit."

"Thanks, I'll watch out for that."

Feeling like an idiot, Raleigh followed him down the hallway toward the garage door. "Griffin."

He turned. "Oh. Ah, hi."

"Are you acting like a bastard on purpose, or is it an accident?" She hadn't meant to come on so strong, but really.

He at least had the good grace to look guilty. "I'm sorry, Raleigh. I wasn't sure what you wanted, but I'm guessing you didn't want to announce to the whole world that we'd had sex."

"No, you're right about that. But a smile or a friendly word wouldn't have been out of place."

"Okay, point taken. But I'm feeling a little confused. What happened this morning—I don't believe it changed anything for you."

How could he think that?

"Well, it apparently changed things for you. You got what you wanted from me, and it's time to move on to the next conquest. Is that it?"

He rolled his eyes. "God, Raleigh, it's not that either. I'm talking about…your situation."

"You mean because I might get killed?" she asked, confused.

"Not that. And you aren't going to get killed. Don't talk that way. I was referring to…to Jason. You're still emotionally attached to him."

"The feelings don't just magically go away."

"I don't expect you to forget him," Griffin said gently. "But I don't think your marriage is over at all. In your heart, you're still with him. You keep his picture with you all the time and at your apartment you have a shrine dedicated to—"

"A *shrine?*"

"Yes, honey, a shrine. That's exactly what it is. I can't compete with a saint. Raleigh, you're a wonderful woman. I don't pretend to know what was going through your head this morning—if anything. I'm happy if I was able to offer you some comfort or release or distraction. But let's leave it at that."

Is that what he thought of their lovemaking? That it meant so little to her? Yes, maybe she hadn't thought it through when she'd started touching him this morning, but—

Why was she arguing with herself, when he was turning to leave?

"Griffin, wait."

"Relax." He turned and pressed a finger to her lips. "Have a low-key day today. If I find out anything, you'll be the first to know. We'll talk later, okay?"

She swallowed the lump in her throat. "Okay."

Then he walked out the door.

Well, that hadn't gone as well as she'd hoped.

She supposed she couldn't heap too much blame on him. She *was* too preoccupied with Jason. And that table in her apartment with all the pictures and the mementos—sometimes she *did* burn a candle there. Maybe it was a shrine.

But she was changing. Or at least, she was willing to change. She had a right to live a full life, and that meant having a man. A partner in life. Okay, maybe even a husband. Jason would never begrudge her that. If he was even watching over her, which she was coming to doubt.

He was probably on some heavenly beach with a bikini babe on each arm. Before he'd started dating her, he'd been quite the player. If he was in heaven now, he wouldn't be living like a monk.

The thought actually made her smile. She didn't

want to think of Jason as eternally yearning for her, miserable.

She was no longer willing to see herself that way, either. She was moving on. She cursed Griffin and blessed him for making her see the light.

"Raleigh?"

Startled, Raleigh whirled around to find Jillian, clipboard in hand, looking worried. "Yes?"

"You have a phone call. Beth has been trying to get hold of you."

"That's odd." Raleigh fished her cell out of her jeans and stared at the blank screen. "Guess I forgot to turn it on," she said sheepishly. It took a whole lot of distraction for her to forget that, but Griffin qualified.

Jillian led Raleigh down a flight of stairs to the basement. Hardly anyone in Houston had a basement. The city was barely above sea level, and anything built underground was damp and seepy. But somehow Daniel had managed.

Managed very well. The lower level was just as luxurious as any other part of the mansion, with thick Oriental carpets and antiqued bronze light fixtures with art glass shades.

"I could have grabbed the extension in the kitchen."

"Anything to do with Project Justice, Daniel is fastidious about privacy. In here. Your call is on line one." Jillian showed her into a private office equipped with the latest computer, a phone, bookshelves, even live plants. And...a window?

Raleigh couldn't resist pulling back the curtain. The window was fake, with its own light source to make it seem as if the sun was shining right outside. Daniel thought of everything.

Jillian closed the door as she left, and Raleigh grabbed the phone and hit the flashing button for line one.

"Hey, Beth, what's up?" She found a pen and notepad.

"Raleigh! I'm so glad nothing happened to you. You could have been killed! Is Griffin really okay?"

"He is now. He claims it's a minor wound." Raleigh shuddered. "I'll tell him you asked." If she ever spoke to him again. She was awash in confusion where Griffin was concerned.

"I'm really relieved. But that's not the only reason I called. I'm afraid I have some bad news."

What now? Raleigh sank into the leather chair behind the desk. "Lay it on me."

"Lieutenant Comstock called. It seems he can't find the bullet that killed Michelle Brewster."

*"What?"*

"He says he found the evidence files, but the bullet is missing. With closed cases, where they have a conviction, sometimes things get tossed or lost. He says it happens all the time."

"It does happen all the time, but it shouldn't. Of all the incompetent, slovenly, careless, idiotic…" She ran out of adjectives.

This was her whole case. The bullet comparison could have proved that gun was the murder weapon, Raleigh was sure of it. And then she would have been able to track the gun to someone other than Anthony.

"I'm sorry, Raleigh. Lieutenant Comstock sounded frustrated and angry about it, too, so don't come down too hard on him."

"Beth, you're way too trusting. Comstock is probably dancing a jig as we speak. He doesn't want us to exonerate Anthony. He probably pocketed the bullet himself, and now it's at the bottom of Buffalo Bayou. What about tracing the gun registration? Any progress there?"

"He said they were working on it."

"How long does it take? You plug some numbers into a computer and it spits out the answer." She knew it wasn't quite that easy, since the number had been incomplete. But if she could get a list of names— a hundred names, five hundred names—she would have somewhere to start looking.

"Why don't you ask Mitch to run the number?"

Because it would be illegal. Project Justice was not a law-enforcement agency and they didn't have legitimate access to the ATF database. But Mitch probably knew how to get in, or he had a friend somewhere who could help. If it led her to a suspect…

"Never mind," Beth said. "You're an officer of the court and all that."

Which meant Beth would ask Mitch herself.

Fine, Raleigh wouldn't discourage her. She was desperate.

"Do you know when you'll be back in the office?" Beth asked.

Raleigh sighed. "When Daniel says it's okay."

The office door opened and Jillian stood there, looking frantic and apologetic all at the same time.

"I have to go, Beth. I'll call you later." She hung up and focused on Jillian. "Trouble?"

"Daniel wants to see you right away."

*Now* what? Raleigh followed Jillian down the hall to another door. When she entered Daniel's office— his lair, some people called it—her eyes almost popped out of her head.

She'd heard about this place, but she'd never actually been here until today.

It looked less an office and more a control center. Or the deck of the *Starship Enterprise*. She counted four TVs, mounted high on the walls, all of them broadcasting multiple screens of a news program. A huge, U-shaped desk dominated the room; it held two computers plus a small laptop. Daniel sat in the center, actually typing on two keyboards at once, one with each hand. He also had a Bluetooth headset in his ear.

He looked up when she entered. "Raleigh. Come in, please. Sit down." His face looked grim.

On the periphery of the huge desk were several comfortable chairs. She chose one at random and sat. "Is someone hurt? They didn't go after my parents, did they?" Her parents lived far away, in Iowa, but anything was possible.

"No, it's nothing like that. But I'm afraid you've become the subject of some sensational press coverage. The story came over CNI a few minutes ago. I record everything continuously with DVRs on a twenty-four-hour loop, in case I need to review a report—like this."

He pointed to one of the TV screens, rewinding through a recording until he got to the segment he wanted.

A sober-looking woman began her report with a hint of relish. "Project Justice, the Houston foundation that frees those unjustly convicted, is embroiled in yet another controversial case—this one involving notorious crime-family member Anthony Simonetti, currently on death row for the brutal murder of his girlfriend, Michelle Brewster."

Oh, no. Raleigh had known it was only a matter of time before the media glommed on to this story, but it still disturbed her, especially given the bad news she'd just received.

"At the center of this case is attorney Raleigh Shinn, who only a few weeks ago successfully argued to free convicted millionaire Eldon Jasperson when his son—whom he supposedly murdered—turned up alive and well."

A rather unflattering photo of Raleigh flashed on the screen. Did she really look like that?

"Regarding the Simonetti case, the supposed murder weapon has turned up, and Shinn is shepherding the evidence through a series of high-tech analyses, confident the results will prove her client, the son of notorious 'machete man' Leo Simonetti, is innocent."

Raleigh's picture was replaced with one of Leo Simonetti, who had absolutely nothing to do with this case.

Raleigh held her breath, knowing the worst was to come.

"But apparently not everyone is pleased with Shinn's efforts. She's been the target of threatening phone calls, and late last night, Shinn's apartment was showered with gunfire, shattering the windows and injuring a guest staying at Shinn's home."

"Inaccurate," Raleigh said. "Only one phone call. And Griffin wasn't 'staying' with me."

"But some have asked exactly what has motivated Shinn to pursue this case so relentlessly. A source close to the case reports that Shinn has received payments—tens of thousands of dollars—from a

Swiss bank account, and that she has been in almost constant communication with Leo Simonetti."

Raleigh was out of her chair. "Oh, my God."

"Shinn was not answering her phone as of this morning."

"Because my apartment is a crime scene! Exactly how hard did they try to get hold of me?"

The anchor moved on to another story and Daniel switched off the TV. "This report is libelous. Jillian is trying to get hold of someone at CNI as we speak. I'm asking for an immediate retraction."

"Daniel, you know I haven't been receiving kick-backs, right? And that I've never talked with Leo Simonetti in my life?"

"Raleigh, of course. You don't even have to ask. I'm more concerned about this 'source close to the story.'"

"You think it's Griffin?" The possibility was almost unspeakable.

"Who else knew the details of the deposit? And the falsified phone records?"

"I told Beth…no, that's ridiculous. She would never betray a confidence."

"I trusted him." Daniel shook his head. "I'm usually a good judge of character. But I was obviously wrong about Griffin Benedict. It's not just that he violated his word. That would be bad enough. But he's passed on to the network information that he knows to be false."

"I can't believe he would do that."

"You have…feelings for this man?"

She wanted to lie, but she couldn't. Not to Daniel. "I did. Now, I want to shoot the son of a bitch through the heart."

## CHAPTER THIRTEEN

GRIFFIN FELT like a jerk for the way he'd treated Raleigh earlier that morning. But he could see no future for them, and it seemed less cruel in the long run to break things off cleanly.

His heart was in physical pain whenever he thought of never seeing her again. He'd become attached to her in such a short time. But he refused to be part of a threesome—himself, Raleigh and St. Jason.

That Jason was one lucky son of a gun, even if he was dead. Hell, Griffin must have been pretty far gone if he could be envious of a dead man.

Now, Griffin's only priority was to finish what he'd started. He needed to see this story to its conclusion, publish it, then try to expunge memories of Raleigh and their lovemaking form his mind.

Finishing the story meant finding out who wanted to kill Raleigh. Which was why he was in an old-fashioned barbershop downtown—not far from the Project Justice offices, actually—with hot towels on his face, preparing to get a shave and a haircut.

If his sources were right, Leo Simonetti would shortly be sitting in the chair next to his. Leo came once a week, like clockwork, to Sam's Barbershop, for his regular trim, shave and manicure.

There seemed no other way to get access to Leo. Although he was the CEO of a legitimate business, a car-leasing outfit aimed at executives, you couldn't get in to see Leo unless he knew you. And he liked reporters even less than did Daniel Logan.

Sam's had three barbers and a manicurist on staff this morning, and the place seemed to be doing a steady business. Maybe it was the nostalgia factor. Maybe there were others waiting to meet Leo.

Griffin heard a flurry of activity coming from the direction of the front door.

"Mr. S! How good to see you." It was the voice of the shop's obsequious owner, whose name was Enrico, not Sam. "The usual today?"

"Think I'll have one of those avocado things on my face, too," Leo Simonetti said. "My skin seems a little dry."

Funny, hearing a man who'd killed an enemy with a machete and cut him up into small pieces requesting an avocado face mask. But he was wealthy, and wealthy people could afford to be pampered.

Griffin peeked out from beneath his hot towel and saw Leo Simonetti in person for the first time. He was shorter than Griffin had pictured him, and very round, though his well-tailored suit disguised his girth. He stripped off his jacket, and another man, who must have been a bodyguard, took the jacket and draped it over a chair in the area where people waiting for haircuts sat.

Leo didn't wait, of course, since he had a standing appointment. He showed himself to the chair to Griffin's left.

The barber, Enrico himself, fastened a cape around Leo's neck, then leaned his chair back and applied a hot towel to his face.

"Yow. Enrico, what are you trying to do, send me to the burn unit?"

"Just trying to give you a nice, smooth shave, how you like." Enrico sounded unperturbed, as if maybe this dialogue was a comforting routine they went through every week.

"Mr. Simonetti?" Griffin injected what he thought was just the right amount of respect and awe.

"Who wants to know?"

"My name is Griffin Benedict. Wow, I can't believe I'm sitting right next to you."

"You're a reporter." Leo sounded disgusted.

Griffin was unnerved to realize he was on the radar of a homicidal mobster. Coincidence? Or did he know exactly who Griffin was because of his interest in Raleigh?

"Have to earn a living somehow," Griffin said, trying to make light of Leo's negative feelings toward the press. "Don't worry, I'm not writing a story about you."

"Good. 'Cause if I hear the words 'machete man' coming out of your mouth—"

Enrico pulled the towel off Griffin's face. "Mr. Simonetti is my best customer. I don't stand for him being badgered in my place."

Leo laughed. "Ah, leave the kid alone, Rico."

"I don't mean to cause you any trouble, Mr. Simonetti," Griffin said as another barber, whose name tag identified him as Theo, lathered up Griffin's face. "But I'm curious how you feel about the possibility of your son's conviction being overturned."

Leo whipped the towel off his face and sat up, focusing his infamous laserlike black eyes on Griffin. "They're gonna let Luigi go? Since when?"

Luigi was Leo's oldest son, doing ten to twenty for bank fraud. Griffin observed Leo out the corner of his eye. "Ah, not Luigi. Anthony."

"Anthony." A different expression came over Leo's face. Griffin would almost call it tender. "He don't talk to me no more. But I knew all along he didn't do it. That gun they found—I bet they traced it to Little Louie. Am I right?"

Who the hell was Little Louie? "All I heard was they might have found the murder weapon, and they might be able to tie it to someone other than Anthony."

Theo sharpened his straight razor on a strop. Griffin was acutely aware of how vulnerable he was, surrounded by a mob leader and his protective friends.

"I already know that much," Leo said. "A man in my position hears things."

Not surprising. Leo probably had plants at the police department. Every good mobster had a few cops on his payroll. Sad but true fact.

"Of course, Anthony doesn't tell me. Like I said, he don't talk to me." Leo sounded put out.

Enrico soothed the mobster back into the chair and lathered up his face.

"But that gun they found," Leo continued, "it's not Anthony's, that's for damn sure. Kid would never touch a gun. Even when he was little. 'Guns are bad, Papa.' He would cry if he even saw one. Sometimes I wonder how I sired that kid. But I still love him."

Griffin actually felt for the guy. His paternal feelings seemed genuine.

"So, Mr. Smart Guy Reporter, you think this gun thing might pan out? He might get out of jail?"

"I don't know all the details, just that there's a possibility. Who's Little Louie?"

"Louis Costanza. Nutcase. His father, Christophe, is someone I do business with. A few years ago I got a little irritated with Christophe 'cause he delivered some counterfeit auto parts to my mechanic. Supposed to be Mercedes, German crafted, and instead he shows up with Chinese fakes. So maybe I didn't pay him and he got irritated right back at me.

"But Christophe and I, we go way back, we work things out. Louie, though, the son, he's a whack job.

Thinks he'll earn some brownie points with the father by getting even with me, shooting my son."

"Except Anthony wasn't home," Griffin concluded. "But his girlfriend was."

"You got it." Then, more to himself, he added, "So wrong, on every level."

Holy hell. Was Leo telling the truth? "Do you know for sure Louie did it?"

Theo ran the straight razor cleanly around Griffin's chin. The blade was so sharp it felt like a satin ribbon.

"Louie couldn't keep his mouth shut."

"The police never named him as a suspect."

"The police weren't interested in my theories about my son's girlfriend's murderer. They said I was unreliable, that I was just making stuff up. But, you know, what goes around comes around. Few weeks later, Louie died behind the wheel. Driving drunk."

A convenient accident. "But Anthony still paid the price."

"He wouldn't accept my help. Pigheaded like his mother, that one."

If Griffin had been in Anthony's shoes, maybe he wouldn't have accepted the gangster's help, either. Leo's brand of help might have involved bribing a judge or engaging in a bit of jury tampering, which could have exploded in Anthony's face.

"Have you talked to Anthony?" Leo asked. He sounded thirsty for any news of his son.

"No. Just to one of his lawyers." Griffin was loath to bring Raleigh or Project Justice to Leo's attention if he didn't already know about them.

"If you talk to him, tell him all's forgiven."

"I will."

"And you write one word of this conversation in your stinking newspaper, I'll cut off your family jewels and stuff them down your throat."

Griffin tried to swallow, but his mouth had gone suddenly dry. Why was everyone threatening his private parts? "No worries about that." As of this morning, he no longer worked for the *Telegram*. He'd had a difficult conversation with his longtime editor, Marvin Gussler—told him everything. To his credit, Marvin hadn't gotten mad. But then, nothing much ever ruffled the guy. He'd told Griffin to take a leave of absence, give it a week, then decide. Marvin had even hinted that a raise wouldn't be out of the question.

Now, at the barbershop, Griffin didn't say another word, and he prayed for Theo to finish his work quickly.

"He's at the front gate. Should we let him in?" Jillian, clipboard in hand, had just entered the dining room where Daniel and Raleigh were having a late lunch—tuna salad on fresh, crusty croissants right out of the oven. The delicious bread stuck in Raleigh's throat.

Daniel set down his tea. "By all means, let him in. Let's see what he has to say for himself."

Raleigh cleared her throat. "Maybe I should go make myself busy."

"Nonsense. Raleigh, I never took you for a coward. Face the bastard head-on. Don't let him see you hurting."

Wise words. But Raleigh wasn't sure she could follow the advice. Already, her chest felt tight and her eyes burned, and she hadn't even seen Griffin yet.

Still, she couldn't leave. Her boss had given her a direct order. She'd never seen Daniel in his dangerous mode, and she made a note never to cross the man. She wouldn't want to be in Griffin's shoes.

A couple of minutes later, Griffin strode into the dining room as if he owned the place. He didn't even have the good grace to show remorse.

And he looked incredible. He'd gotten a *haircut?* At a time like this?

"You have a lot of nerve," Daniel said with deceptive mildness.

Griffin looked confused. Not rueful. "You already know?"

"Of course we know. CNI runs continuous news feeds all day long. You didn't think they would sit on a juicy story like that for more than a few minutes, did you?"

"Wait…how would CNI know anything about my meeting with Leo Simonetti?"

Now it was Daniel's turn to look confused. Jillian, too. And Raleigh was pretty sure her own consternation radiated out of her like a lighthouse beacon.

"You met with Leo?" Raleigh couldn't help asking. "God, Griffin, the man is a cold-blooded killer."

"A killer who loves his son. He's not the one trying to stop you from exonerating Anthony. He would like nothing better than to see his boy free and back in the bosom of his family. Now, your turn. What story are you all talking about?"

"The whole story is out," Daniel said through clenched teeth. "Finding the gun, our attempt to free Anthony, Raleigh's stalker. Everything."

"Griffin," Raleigh said, unable to hold her tongue, "I would have understood if you'd just written the story. Journalism is your calling, not to mention your livelihood, and you have a lot riding on reporting this situation. But the spin you gave it—I thought you believed me when I said I wasn't accepting bribes—"

Griffin held up his hand. "Stop. I have no idea what you're talking about."

"You don't know anything about a certain story that broke on CNI this morning, shortly after you left? And you wouldn't be the anonymous 'source close to the investigation'?"

With every word she spoke, Griffin's face got

harder. "I haven't written any stories. Not for CNI or the *Telegram*."

"No one else knew the details in the story," Raleigh said quietly, trying not to cry. If he would just admit he'd done it, that he'd fallen prey to greed or weakness, maybe she could have dealt with it, found some way to forgive him. But to stand there and deny he was involved—convincingly, she might add...

"What details?" Griffin demanded.

Daniel intervened. "The deposit from a Swiss bank account. The supposed phone calls to Leo Simonetti. Falsified phone bill. Tests being done on the gun. The phone threat. Only four people knew all of the details, and I'm pretty sure Beth, Raleigh and I didn't speak with anyone at CNI."

Griffin's eyes hardened to chips of granite. "You're forgetting one other person who knew everything. The man who's behind all this. I have no idea what he hopes to accomplish with heightened publicity, but I'm damn sure going to find out."

He looked at Daniel and Raleigh in turn, daring both of them to continue their accusations. Raleigh didn't have the nerve. If anything, an angry Griffin was more intimidating than Daniel at his most deadly. But she was surprised Daniel had nothing to add to the argument.

"I came back here to tell you something. I have a lead for you. The name of the man who might actually have killed Anthony's girlfriend. Louis Costanza, aka 'Little Louie.' Apparently he chose an odd way of settling a score between his father and Leo."

Raleigh struggled to get her mind up to speed, processing the startling new information. "You're saying this Louis might be the one trying to stop me from exonerating Anthony?"

"Probably not, since he's dead." Griffin turned to leave.

"Wait, where are you going?" Raleigh asked. She couldn't just let him leave like this.

He turned, and the look he gave her chilled her blood. "I'm gonna do what I set out to do—find the person who's trying to hurt you and put a stop to it. Then, I doubt you'll see me again."

Daniel, Raleigh and Jillian took turns staring at one another for a good thirty seconds after Griffin cleared the room.

Finally, Daniel broke the stunned silence. "Of course. If it wasn't Griffin, it had to be the real villain."

Raleigh tried to work through it. "When Griffin wouldn't take the bait, my stalker found some other reporter to tarnish my reputation."

"Well, he's not going to get away with it," Daniel said fiercely. "Jillian, get someone on the phone at CNI. Someone capable of making a decision."

"I've left three messages already this morning."

"This time, get through to them. Tell them their 'anonymous source' might well have tried to kill

Raleigh. And if they don't hand over his name—to the police, if not to me—they could get slapped with an Obstruction of Justice charge."

"I like it," Jillian said with a smile before departing.

"Come on, Raleigh," Daniel said when they were alone. "Smile. This is coming to a head, and soon. Your enemy is getting desperate. His plan is unraveling. He'll make a big mistake soon, and then this will all be over."

Raleigh didn't feel much like smiling, despite the fact that Griffin had just handed her a huge bone. Louis Costanza? The name meant nothing to her.

"Daniel, I know I'm supposed to be on vacation, but I need to follow up on the name Griffin supplied."

"You have an office with a phone, computer and internet at your disposal. Let me know what I can do."

A SHORT TIME LATER, Raleigh had a boatload of information on Louis Costanza. He was, indeed, the son of Christophe Costanza, a dealer in auto parts who was purported to be a minor cog in Leo Simonetti's crime family. Unfortunately, the son had been killed in a drunk driving accident just two weeks after Michelle Brewster's murder.

Raleigh spoke with the detective who had investigated that accident. He'd been harboring misgivings about it for years because something hadn't "felt right" about it.

"Like it might have been staged?" Raleigh had asked.

"Yeah. One-car accident. Car hit a light post. Victim had enough alcohol in his blood that he shouldn't have been able to find his car keys, much less drive the car seventeen miles from where he'd last been seen alive. A surprising amount of trauma to his body, given the specifics of the accident."

"But I couldn't get my teeth into anything."

The scenario made sense. If Louie had killed Michelle as revenge against Leo, someone might have evened the score. Leo himself could be responsible. He might have had Louie killed, not realizing he'd put the nail in his own son's coffin.

After ending her conversation with the detective, Raleigh was still stumped. Who else, besides Michelle's actual killer, wanted to stop Raleigh from exonerating Anthony? Was it some mob vendetta thing?

Her cell phone rang. Caller ID was blocked, which gave her pause. But curiosity got the better of her. "Raleigh Shinn."

"Raleigh. This is Sergeant Bob Smythe with the Houston Police Department. I have some information for you involving the Anthony Simonetti case."

The name sounded familiar, but she couldn't quite place the man. "You're one of the detectives I've been hounding about running the serial number on that gun?"

"Yes, that's right."

His voice was deep and smooth—the guy sounded like a late-night radio deejay, she caught herself thinking with a smile.

"Did you ID the gun?" she asked excitedly. Please, oh please let it belong to Louis Costanza. Without the bullet match it wasn't a perfect slam dunk, but it would make for a good argument.

"I'd rather not discuss it over the phone. Can you meet me somewhere? I've found another piece of evidence that might be of use to you."

"I can come to headquarters if you like."

"Things are a mess here. Exterminators are here, spraying for cockroaches."

Ew. "How about if I we meet at my office?"

"Perfect. I can be there at five—no, wait. My wife is gonna kill me if I don't get home for dinner on time. Would you mind meeting after hours? Say, seven-thirty?"

"I can do that." It would save her a drive through rush-hour traffic. Daniel would give her the use of a car and probably a bodyguard, too, knowing him. But he wouldn't try to dissuade her from going. Solving this case was too important.

GRIFFIN WAS SO ANGRY he nearly took out a row of privet hedge as he sped down Daniel Logan's

driveway away from the mansion, still in his borrowed car. He would have to find a way to pick up
his Mustang and return Jillian's Range Rover, but
that was the least of his worries.

He couldn't believe CNI had stabbed him in the
back that way. But Raleigh's lack of faith in him was
far more painful. The news network represented a
job, nothing more; Raleigh could have been his whole
future.

Yeah, he was willing to admit it, now that it didn't
matter: he'd fallen in love with her. When he'd tried
to distance himself from her this morning, it hadn't
been because he was jealous of Jason. He'd done it
because on some level he'd been terrified of his own
feelings. He wasn't the kind of guy who fell in love
and spilled his messy emotions all over the place.

But apparently he was, because right now he had
to fight the urge to turn around, drive back up that
mile-long driveway, storm inside the house and tell
Raleigh how he felt.

As angry as he was with her, though, his declara-
tion might not come out just right.

Actions spoke louder than words. The same person
who had initially tried to manipulate him into publishing a libelous story about Raleigh had to be the
same person who had contacted CNI and provided
them with all that bogus information. He doubted
the network would reveal their source to him, and
maybe not even to the cops. Journalists—and he used

the term loosely here—were freakishly protective of sources.

But Griffin had one lead still to follow. He'd called the Johnson-Perrone Medical Center earlier to check on John Shinn's postoperative condition. Raleigh's father-in-law had apparently sailed through the surgery and was doing well. No way would Griffin be allowed to question him. But his wife? She was accessible. Maybe it was time to press Raleigh's mother-in-law about that Swiss bank account.

## CHAPTER FOURTEEN

RALEIGH PICKED at her dinner, anxious about the coming meeting with the detective. Was it possible she had finally convinced the police they'd made a mistake in arresting Anthony in the first place? Police and prosecutors were notoriously slow to admit to mistakes, and Raleigh usually found herself as their adversary.

But they weren't monsters. They could be persuaded. Most of them—the good ones, anyway—wanted the right person behind bars, even if it meant some professional embarrassment.

"You haven't eaten enough of that dinner to keep a bird alive," Daniel observed. He'd been the perfect host, seeing to her every need. He'd even obtained the special food Copper's vet had prescribed for him.

Raleigh smiled. "My dad used to say the same thing to me. I always lose my appetite when I'm nervous."

"You're more than just nervous."

Damn Daniel for being so freaking observant. "Yeah, okay, maybe I'm a little upset over the situation with Griffin, too."

"Romance is one area of my life at which I haven't exactly excelled. So you can take any advice I foist on you with a grain of salt. But I have a feeling he'll come around."

Raleigh had her doubts about that. He'd been so, *so* angry, justifiably so. "Even if he does…I thought we had a chance at first. Griffin made me see that I was limiting myself. He made me feel…happy. For the first time in a long, long time."

"And now you feel like you blew it."

"It's not just that I didn't show any faith in him. Things were going wonky before that. He was the one pulling back, saying it couldn't work for us because I'm still hung up on Jason."

"Are you?"

"I'm not beyond hope! Lately I've been putting things into perspective. But I'm beginning to think Jason was only an excuse. Griffin pushed to get closer to me, and then when he finally did, he didn't want me anymore." And why she was telling this to Daniel Logan, her boss, of all people, she didn't know.

But Daniel was perceptive. Maybe he could help her understand. He might not be in a relationship right now, but he was a man. Surely he understood how the male brain worked better than she did.

She wasn't completely naive when it came to men. She had dated a few, even had some semi-serious boyfriends before she'd met Jason. But regarding Griffin, she felt as baffled as she had in junior high the first time she'd let a boy touch her breast and then he'd bragged about it to anyone who would listen.

Daniel shook his head. "I don't think that's what's going on. I think Griffin Benedict very much wants you. I see it in the way he looked at you. You wounded him today. In the heart."

Raleigh nodded. "As bad as things were, I'm afraid I made them much worse with my accusations. He probably won't even talk to me after this."

"Things often look bleakest just before a stroke of good luck. You can take it from an expert on the subject."

Certainly Daniel had seen some very bleak times. All those years in prison, avoiding a lethal injection by mere days. She should stop feeling sorry for herself. Her prison had been one of her own making, a gilded cage with bars made from idealized memories of her husband.

At least she was free now. She could be grateful to Griffin for that.

THE LIMO PULLED UP in front of the Project Justice building just as the sun set, bathing downtown in a gold-orange glow. A pretty time of day, one Raleigh hardly noticed anymore. But now that her senses had been reawakened, she noticed everything.

"Wait," Randall said when she reached for the door handle. "I'll get that." He would also check out the street and shield her with his own body as he escorted her to the building's front door. Although he posed as a mere chauffeur, Daniel had assured her that Randall had once worked the Presidential detail for the Secret Service.

Ten steps, and she was inside the lobby. Randall said he would park nearby, and she should call him when she was ready to go home.

Raleigh was surprised to see Celeste still at the front desk. Although the lobby stayed open all night, because Project Justice personnel often worked at odd hours, in the evening hours a night watchman was usually on duty.

"You're working late."

"Phil called in sick," she said sourly. "Sick, my sweet patootie. He's watching baseball, I just know it. Daniel's sending someone to relieve me in a while. Till then, I'm stuck here." She punched unhappily at a Mylar Happy Birthday balloon tied to her chair.

Raleigh hadn't even realized Celeste was having a birthday. She really needed to reach out more to people at work. "Sorry. That bites." She set her purse down on the reception desk.

Celeste shrugged. "It's okay. I'll get overtime pay. Thought you were on vacation."

"Only sort of. I'm meeting a sergeant from the police department."

"He's already here. But he stepped outside to have a smoke."

"Hmm." She was sure she hadn't seen anyone

nearby on the street. Raleigh returned to the large double doors and peeked outside. Sure enough, a man in a suit was now leaning against the wall of her building, puffing on the dregs of a cigarette. He must have been stretching his legs a few moments earlier.

He was tall and slender, early forties, maybe, and he sported an enormous handlebar mustache and thick-framed black glasses that seemed out of place on his otherwise pleasant face.

He came instantly alert, straightening his stance. "Raleigh?"

"Yes. You must be Sergeant Smythe."

"Yes, ma'am." As they met halfway on the sidewalk, he reached into an inner pocket, flashed a badge for her, quickly returned it to his jacket, then offered her his hand. "It's nice to see you again."

"I…I'm sorry, have we met?" He did look familiar, but she couldn't quite place him.

"Just once, briefly." He sounded slightly irritated. Normally she was very good with faces and names, but she did meet a lot of law enforcement personnel in the course of her work.

She made a point to shake his hand warmly. Now was her chance to mend some fences. "I'm so glad you called. We don't have time to waste. If Anthony is innocent, he needs to be freed, sooner rather than later." Clearing Anthony's name after he'd died of a lethal injection would be a hollow victory.

"Then you'll want to come with me," the sergeant said. "The evidence I found is in my trunk. I didn't want to just carry it into your office. I know the press is covering you pretty closely."

"I don't want the press to know anything else until I'm good and ready." She started to burn all over again, thinking about that bogus story CNI ran. But she pushed her irritation aside. She had to stay focused.

"My car is parked right around the corner. This is gonna blow your mind."

"Okay, but…" She looked around nervously. This part of downtown Houston became a ghost town after hours, and it was quickly emptying of cars and pedestrians. Also, once the sun set, she wouldn't be able to see much, given her dreadful night vision.

"I *am* a police detective. I've just been checking out the area. I didn't see any suspicious cars or people."

She was being paranoid. She was with one of Houston's finest, as safe as she could be under the circumstances.

"Let's go, then." As they walked, she asked, "So when did we meet?" Surely if she'd met anyone with that distinctive mustache, she would remember.

"We met when you were still working as a defense attorney. I was a witness in one of your trials—for the prosecution."

"Ah. I hope I wasn't too unpleasant toward you."

She was only half joking. Her cross-examinations could get nasty.

Smythe laughed. "You had to do your job. I actually admired your courage."

"If so, you're rare among police."

They stopped at an unmarked Ford Taurus, an anonymous white. Probably picked up at a police auction. So many officers acquired their personal vehicles through the department.

Raleigh's heart started beating faster. She couldn't wait to see what Smythe had to show her. A piece of evidence she didn't know about? Something that tended to rule out Anthony as a suspect, conveniently "lost" by someone in the department to make his job easier?

Something Smythe didn't want to be seen with, or photographed with, which meant it was more than a piece of paper or a folder.

Smythe opened the trunk. Inside was a plain cardboard box, resting toward the back of the large space. The box was old, dusty. On the outside was written, in black marker, *Michelle Brewster P.E.* Physical Evidence.

Raleigh reached for the box. "May I?"

"Help yourself." She pulled open two of the box flaps and leaned in so she could see the contents. Given how dim the lighting was, she had to get close to see.

Suddenly the trunk lid fell and hit her hard on the

back of the head. "Ow! What the—" Before she could even finish a sentence, strong hands clamped around her waist and hauled her off her feet, pushing her into the trunk. She landed painfully on one shoulder as Sergeant Smythe—or whoever he was—folded her legs and stuffed her inside. As she screamed in pain and fury and outrage, he slapped a piece of duct tape over her mouth. She caught just a glimpse of triumph on the man's face—and a crazed look in his eyes— before he slammed the lid shut, trapping her in the darkness.

She rolled over onto her back and beat on the trunk lid with her fists, then kicked with her feet. One of her shoes had fallen off.

"You don't have the slightest idea who I am, do you?" he yelled at her through the trunk. "We met only two days ago."

She scanned her memory banks, coming up blank.

"Don't you ever watch the news?"

Then it came to her. Get rid of the mustache and the glasses, and she was looking at Paul Stratton, anchor of the Channel 6 Evening News, the man who had asked her about John Shinn in the hospital parking lot.

And he wanted her dead because…? Oh, no. Now she saw it. He had been the reporter to break the Michelle Brewster murder story—the first to name Anthony Simonetti a suspect, well before the police had arrested him. He'd earned some kind of award for his series on the case, if she recalled.

If she proved he'd been wrong, his reputation was on the line. But surely the person he most wanted out of the picture was Griffin, his competition for the coveted network job.

He'd been trying to solve two problems with one criminal campaign. Paul could easily have come up with twenty-thousand dollars—news anchors made plenty of money. As a reporter, one people recognized and trusted, he could get at all kinds of information, like bank account numbers and phone bills.

Raleigh screamed again, though she doubted anyone but Paul could hear her. She kicked and beat the trunk lid as the darkness threatened to smother her. But Paul Stratton wasn't about to free her. The fact he had wanted her to know his identity meant he didn't intend for her to live long enough to tell anyone what he'd done. She could only hope someone else would hear her and intervene.

Surely Randall hadn't gone far with the limo. But the Taurus's engine rumbled to life and the car lurched forward. He was getting away with his crime. She was being kidnapped.

She'd heard somewhere that if you were ever kidnapped and thrown into a car trunk, you should kick out the taillights and try to signal someone. But she didn't see any taillights. It was completely dark.

So what did she have to work with? She'd left

her purse, along with her cell phone, on Celeste's desk. The trunk appeared clean, free of any tools or other junk. Except for the box. She quickly found it and reached inside. She found what felt like...bricks. Plain old bricks, probably just to weight the box down so Raleigh would have to lean in farther to grasp it and open it or pull it toward her.

As weapons went, she could do worse than bricks. She pulled two from the box, got a good grip on one in each and concealed them behind her body. When the trunk opened, she would be ready.

GRIFFIN'S ATTEMPT to interview Julia Shinn had been a bust; her secretary said she was "unavailable," and she was nowhere near the hospital. So Griffin had spent his afternoon at home, following up on every lead he had, even the weak ones.

Then he'd resorted to investigating Raleigh's co-workers, including the college interns. Their histories and all private information appeared to have been sanitized. Daniel Logan strikes again.

He was just starting to turn up information on "Little Louie" Costanza when his phone rang. He answered eagerly, half hoping it would be Raleigh.

"Griffin." It was Daniel, sounding all business. "Is Raleigh with you?"

"Why would she be—no."

"I can't locate her."

"She's *missing?*" Every cell in Griffin's body went on high alert.

"She said she was going to the office to meet someone from the Houston P.D.—"

"And you let her go?"

"She's not my prisoner, Griffin," Daniel said a bit testily. "I sent her in the limo with the best bodyguard I have. But Celeste Boggs, who was at the front desk, said the man she was supposed to meet stepped outside for a smoke, and when Raleigh arrived, she went to look for him and never returned."

"And neither did her mysterious contact, I take it."

"No."

"Where was this infamous bodyguard?"

"Parking the limo. Since she was inside the building, he assumed she was safe. So you don't know anything?"

He wanted to scream and curse and reach through the phone to throttle Daniel Logan for being so careless. But that wouldn't bring Raleigh back. "I haven't heard anything, but I'm heading that way now."

"Our security cameras have an image of the guy. He looks familiar, but no one here can place him."

"Can you send it to me?"

"I'll email it to you right now."

Griffin had scarcely disconnected that call when his phone chimed again. Seeing that it was another blocked call, he assumed it was Daniel calling back with more questions.

"What?"

"Benedict." The voice was electronically disguised. "I have something you want."

Griffin stopped dead, his heart slamming into his chest wall. "Do you have Raleigh?"

"There's something you want more than her," the voice said, maddeningly calm.

"No. Nothing is more important than her safety."

"What about…the story? The big story. The one that will get you the job with the seven-figure paycheck. You want that more than anything, don't you, Benedict?"

"What do you want?" Griffin demanded.

"No, my friend, the correct question is, what do *you* want? If you want to see your girlfriend alive ever again, you'll do exactly as I tell you. No police. No Project Justice. Not if you want an exclusive. But if you follow my directions to a T, I'll give you the interview of your life. You'll never have a chance at a story like this again."

As if he cared about that! "Let me talk to Raleigh."

"You'll have to trust me—she is alive and well. A bit uncomfortable, perhaps—"

"You bastard! If you hurt her I'll hunt you down and shoot you in the street like a rabid dog."

"Do you want to see her again or no?"

Griffin reined in his temper. The man behind the

tinny voice was trying to upset him. Best not to play his game.

"Just tell me where to find her."

"There's an alley just west of the Project Justice office. It's overgrown with weeds and rusty Dumpsters. A nice, dark place to finish our business."

"I'll find it. But listen, you have to promise me—"

The line went dead.

So, Raleigh's kidnapper thought Griffin's ego was so big, that he wanted this story so badly, he would risk Raleigh's life? Dream on. Griffin would call in the police, the FBI, the frigging National Guard—whatever it took. Honest to God, who cared about the damn story?

But then he had a better idea. As he headed for his car, which he'd parked in the street in front of his town house, he dialed Daniel's number.

"Daniel. He called me. He told me where to find Raleigh."

To his credit, Daniel didn't doubt Griffin's word or demand details. "Should I contact the police?"

Griffin quickly filled Daniel in on the specifics of the anonymous phone call, and the directions the man had given.

"You'd be crazy to meet him alone," Daniel said. "He'll kill you both. He might be trying to set up some sort of murder-suicide scenario."

"I don't plan to be alone. But I want Project Justice

behind me. I'd rather have a handful of your people backing me up than the cops. You can mobilize faster, you'll know exactly when to intervene—and I won't have to spend an hour explaining things to you. Can you do it?"

"Absolutely," Daniel said without hesitation. "But I'll alert law enforcement, as well. I have contacts there who will take me at my word. I'll have a plan and some backup for you in fifteen minutes. Can you wait until then?"

"Yes." It would be insane to go blundering into the kidnapper's trap. But this would be the longest fifteen minutes Griffin had ever lived through.

RALEIGH HEARD the trunk lock turn, and she braced herself for the next assault. But night had fallen during the few minutes she'd been trapped in the trunk, so what she got was a flashlight in the face, momentarily blinding her.

"How are you doing in there?"

In reply, Raleigh screamed. But with her mouth taped shut, she couldn't create any volume.

"Enough of that. I don't want you announcing your whereabouts until I'm ready. You should be comforted to know your boyfriend is on his way. Be a good girl, don't give me any trouble, and soon the two of you will be together again."

*Griffin?* Is that who he meant? *Oh, Griffin, it's a trap. Don't come.*

She still had the use of her hands. And she had her bricks. But she didn't have much time; Paul was about to close the trunk on her again. In a panic, she lobbed one of the bricks at him. It bounced off his shoulder, getting his attention but doing no harm.

"You little bitch!" He grabbed her right arm. She tried to kick at him but she was wildly ineffective. He was stronger than he looked.

With the remaining brick in her left hand she tried to hit his hands, to break his grip on her. His response was to backhand her across the face and grab the brick, tossing it aside.

While she reeled from the blow, eyes stinging and nose running, he wrapped her wrists in duct tape.

*No!* He was not going to leave her helpless in this dark trunk again. Her nose was bleeding; she could barely breathe. She had to do something. She had to stop Griffin from trying to rescue her.

Raleigh made one more effort to use her feet. Her left foot still wore a black pump. Not as useful as a stiletto heel might have been, but it had a hard sole. She brought her knee up as high as it would go, then aimed carefully for Paul's midsection and kicked as hard as she could.

This time she made contact. With an audible *oof* he let go of her hands and backed away. She swung her legs over the lip of the trunk and levered herself out.

Paul made a grab for her and got a handful of her hair.

She screamed and kicked backward, connecting with something hard. His grip loosened just enough that she could pull away, and she started running.

## CHAPTER FIFTEEN

PAUL STRATTON CURSED, but he let her go because he knew she couldn't get far. Running blindly, she'd headed farther into the alley. Soon she would discover there was no way out—no way but up. He'd pulled the fire escape stairs down, easily within her reach, anticipating just this scenario, although without the blow to his stomach.

Once she went up, she would be trapped.

He slammed the trunk lid, jumped into his car and backed wildly out of the alley. He had no way of knowing how far away Benedict was, but he needed to get ready for the confrontation. A six-foot-plus male would be a bit more of a challenge than a lady lawyer in one shoe, though she'd shown more strength—and backbone—than he'd expected. His ribs would be bruised for a week.

He parked his car at the first available spot on the street, yanked off the fake mustache, glasses and hat, then jumped out of the car and ducked back into the alley. No sign of Raleigh. She was either hiding somewhere, in some weeds or behind a Dumpster, or she'd gone up. Either way, she was still trapped.

He watched the street, waiting for Benedict's Mustang to come tearing toward him. He couldn't wait to get the guy alone. Benedict's huge ego would be his undoing. He had a reputation for going anywhere and doing anything for a story.

This was one story he wouldn't write—unless he could write from the grave.

Gradually, Paul became aware of a police siren. Not unusual in this urban area. But it got louder. And louder. Then he saw the flashing lights, heading this way.

Crap. Had Benedict actually alerted the police? Or had someone realized Raleigh was missing?

No, the cops wouldn't come blazing in here just because no one had seen the lawyer for a few minutes.

Benedict had caved. He'd been unselfish, for once in his life. Amazing.

Paul held out one final hope that the cops were heading somewhere else. But the black-and-white pulled right up to the Project Justice building.

Heart pounding, he knew he had just one chance to get this right. He ran up to the police cruiser as two uniforms climbed out.

"Thank goodness. He took her. He just grabbed her and stuffed her into the trunk!" Paul did his best to sound hysterical. He'd minored in theater while in college; he could play this role easy enough. Dancing back and forth from foot to foot, he pointed frantically down the street.

"Calm down, sir," the patronizing officer said. "What did you see?"

Paul made as if to calm himself, breathing deeply, one hand holding his chest. "A man with a hat and a big mustache. He was walking with a woman—she had on jeans and a shirt—no, a sweater—and they were walking down the sidewalk. He stopped and opened the trunk of his car—"

"What kind of car?"

"A...it was black, I think. A sedan. I...I don't remember. But it had Oklahoma plates, I remember that! He grabbed the woman and stuffed her in the trunk, and then he drove off!"

"Which way did he go?" one cop asked.

"When did this happen?" the other one asked.

They couldn't have done a better Mutt and Jeff routine if they'd tried. "It just happened. Two or three minutes ago. He went that way and turned right at the light."

One officer relayed the information into a radio; the other continued to pepper Paul with questions.

"What are you doing here? Can I get some ID?" a young, beefy cop asked.

Another slug living under a rock who didn't recognize him. "Yes, of course. I was on my way home. I work in that building—" He pointed vaguely up the street. "I was headed to my car. I still can't believe it!"

He showed the cop a bogus driver's license he kept around for just such an occasion. "Please." Paul injected as much desperation into his voice as he could. "Please, you have to help that woman."

"Come on, let's go," the beefy cop's partner said. "We have a sighting of the car."

Really? A car Paul had just made up? That was fortunate. How many black sedans with Oklahoma plates were trolling the Houston streets?

Moments later, the police cruiser sped off in the direction the mythical car had taken.

That had been remarkably easy. Amazing how people liked and trusted him on sight. That, plus some damn good acting, had sent the police on a wild-goose chase.

Now, to find out what his prey was up to.

SHE'D GOTTEN AWAY! A surge of triumph coursed through Raleigh's veins as she kicked off her remaining shoe and ran in bare feet down the dark alley.

But her elation was short-lived when she realized there was no way out. The alley ended at a chain-link fence topped with razor wire.

Why wasn't Paul following her? Had she hurt him that badly?

If she turned around and went back the way she'd come, she would run right into him. And he had the advantage of good eyesight: hers was rapidly failing in the twilight. She could make out general shapes, but the details were lost. She had to hide or find another way out.

She'd heard a siren a few moments ago and hope had sprung into her being. But shortly after, the siren had started up again, then moved farther away. She wasn't going to be rescued by the police.

Climbing the fence was no good. She wasn't an action hero; that razor wire would slash her to ribbons before she could clear it. She eyed the hulking shape of a Dumpster, then the zigzag shape of a fire escape. If she could get inside one of the upper floors of this building…the Project Justice building, she realized, and her heart sank. No way could she get inside. Security was too tight. Probably no way to alert anyone inside the building. The windows were all dark at this end.

"Raleigh? Where are you?" The question came in a singsong voice, drifting down the dark alley, and her blood went cold.

She had to act now. Dumpster, or fire escape?

The fire escape won. It was a few feet off the ground, but reachable. She pulled herself up onto the metal stairs, her adrenaline giving her the strength of an Olympic gymnast. Then she climbed, as quickly and quietly as she could. Three flights, and she was as high as she could go. She chanced a look down and saw Paul—or something—moving up the alley toward her at a leisurely pace, as if he had nothing to worry about.

If he looked up, he would see her, and she would be an easy target. If there was something to hide behind...

That was when she saw the ladder that went to the roof. That was her only choice—farther up.

Her hands were slippery with sweat. She wiped them on her jeans then started the climb, expecting a bullet to slam into her body at any time. But luck was with her. She climbed onto the gravel-and-tar roof of the building. The gravel bit through her bare feet, but the pain hardly registered.

She couldn't go anywhere from here—the fire escape was the one route down. But she had places to hide—big air-conditioning units, some ancient chimneys from an era when the residents of this old building had burned coal to stay warm.

Or, she could signal someone.

Unfortunately, it seemed everyone who worked on this entire block had gone home on time today. She peeked over the low wall toward the parking lot behind the building: deserted. She ran toward the street side, always keeping an eye toward the fire escape ladder, expecting to see Paul appear there any second.

So far, it seemed he hadn't figured out where she'd gone.

She peeked over the low wall to the street. Empty. Not a single inhabited car, as if it were the middle of the night instead of a normal weekday evening.

There, she saw headlights at the end of the block. But would the driver see her?

She jumped up and down and waved her arms as the car approached, resisting the urge to scream out for help, because that would alert Paul to her whereabouts.

The car…it was slowing down. Yesss! Then she realized it wasn't just any car. It was a black Mustang. Her hopes plummeted.

"No, Griffin," she whispered. What was he doing? Of course, he didn't yet know he was as much a target as she was. Maybe he thought he was coming to her aid, or maybe Paul had brought him here with some other ruse. Either way, Griffin had no idea his life was at risk.

The Mustang pulled in front of Project Justice and stopped, but Griffin didn't turn off the engine or get out. He was waiting for something. Anytime he wanted, Paul could shoot him through the windshield. Griffin was a sitting duck. She had to warn him.

Raleigh looked all around for some means to signal Griffin without also calling Paul's attention to her. Then she saw—or rather, felt—the answer. She stooped down and grabbed a handful of gravel.

With a silent apology to the mirror finish on Griffin's beautiful car, she lobbed her handful of gravel at it. The small rocks showered the car with a satisfying rattle.

The driver's door opened immediately and Griffin jumped out, looking up. He had a gun in his hand.

"Griffin. You have to get out of here."

"Raleigh? Thank God—"

She was grabbed from behind, and pulled away from the edge of the rooftop. A strong hand clamped over her mouth as Paul put a gun to her head.

"Come get her, Benedict," he called out in a husky, gritty voice that wasn't quite his own, then laughed softly.

GRIFFIN'S HEART nearly forced itself into his mouth. Raleigh, her face covered in blood, and a man. Griffin had seen him, in shadow, for only a few seconds. But something about him was familiar. The stance, the silhouette of a full head of hair…and that voice. It rubbed against him like sandpaper, like—

Suddenly the answer came to him with sickening clarity. Raleigh was not, and never had been, the target. Raleigh had been a means to an end.

Griffin himself was the one Paul Stratton had wanted to hurt—first by trying to lure him into publishing a bogus story that would hurt his reputation. Then, when that didn't work, by outright killing him. The bullet that had come within inches of his heart had never been meant for Raleigh.

"Don't hurt her, Paul," Griffin warned. "This is between you and me." What had been a professional rivalry had become a life-and-death struggle, as if

they were two gladiators in an arena, the loser to be
eaten by lions.

"Come get her," Paul challenged again, now speaking in his normal voice. He was well back from the
edge of the roof, where Griffin couldn't see him. "If
I see anyone but you coming up that fire escape, you
can kiss Raleigh goodbye."

Griffin looked around frantically. Where were the
cops? Where were the Project Justice people?

His phone rang, and he answered it as he made
his way to the alley.

"Benedict here."

"Raleigh's been taken hostage." It was Daniel.
"The police have a witness who saw her taken—"

"She's right here, Daniel," Griffin interrupted.
"She's on the roof of your own goddamn building.
The kidnapper is Paul Stratton. I'm going in."

"Wait, Griffin—"

He couldn't wait for reinforcements. Every second
Raleigh was in the hands of this crazed man was another second of mortal danger. Stratton was insane—
surely he didn't think he could get away with his mad
plan now.

Unless he killed both Raleigh and Griffin. Made
it look like a lover's quarrel gone deadly…yes, that
had to be what he had in mind. Even their deaths
wouldn't stop the freight train of Stratton's downfall,
but he was obviously too unbalanced to see that.

Stratton expected him to go up the fire escape.

The moment his head cleared the roof, Stratton would shoot it off. There had to be another way.

Quickly he reversed his steps and rang the night bell at the Project Justice front door.

"Who is it?" came Celeste's voice.

"Griffin Benedict. Celeste, Raleigh is being held hostage—"

The door buzzed and Griffin burst in. Celeste was already on her feet and, God help them all, she was holding the biggest handgun he'd ever seen—had to be a .50 caliber.

"I knew that fake cop was up to no good!" she declared.

"They're on the roof," Griffin said urgently. "How can we get up there besides the fire escape?"

Suddenly Celeste was all steely efficiency. "Down the hall, up the stairs." She tossed him some keys. "The brass one with the round head opens the hatch to the roof." She turned and headed for the front door.

"Where are you going?"

"Gonna create a diversion." She grabbed one of the Mylar balloons tied to her chair, then took off toward the front door. The woman had to be in her seventies, but she could run like a gazelle even in her high-heeled boots. The flowers on her ridiculous hat bounced with every step.

Griffin didn't have time to try to stop her. A diversion? What the hell did she meant to do? God forgive him for endangering an elderly lady, even if she was, by all accounts, a competent ex-cop and tough as a sledgehammer.

He barreled down the hallway and up the stairs two at a time. Three flights, and he reached the hatch. Brass key. Round head. The lock turned.

Griffin paused long enough to yank off his boots and socks—he would be quieter in bare feet. He opened the hatch two inches and peeked out. He could see them. Stratton still had his hand over Raleigh's mouth, his gun pointed at her head as he held her against him like a shield and faced the fire escape, watching intently.

There was no way Griffin could get off a safe shot. Stratton left no part of his anatomy exposed for long, not from this angle. Even if Griffin shot him cleanly, Stratton's hand might jerk and pull his own trigger, killing Raleigh.

Griffin spotted movement in the building across the street. He crossed his fingers that Daniel's people had arrived. Not that they could stop Stratton if he suddenly tired of the game.

If anyone was going to rescue Raleigh, it had to be Griffin.

Slowly he opened the trapdoor a few more inches, enough that he could crawl through. Recalling his days of battlefield reporting, he moved silently as a cat, mindful that the slightest movement would cause the gravel to crunch.

Raleigh looked over and saw him. Her eyes widened and he froze, gun ready, in case she accidentally alerted Stratton. But the reporter's attention was firmly on the fire escape.

"Benedict?" Stratton called out. "I'm not gonna wait forever for you to make your move. I'll give you one more minute. Then your girl is history, and I'm coming after you. Your only chance to save her is to fight with me, one on one—if you're man enough."

Griffin didn't believe it for a second. Stratton didn't intend for either of his targets to live beyond the next couple of minutes to tell the tale.

Griffin made his way, duckwalking slowly when he wanted to run, the gravel biting into his bare feet. Finally he reached some cover behind an air-conditioning unit. He fell back on his martial arts training, breathing slowly, deeply but quietly, taking in as much oxygen as possible.

That was when he heard a noise on the fire escape. Oh, God. Not Celeste. Please.

Something rose above the roofline—hard to tell what it was in the darkness. It looked like…Celeste's flowered hat.

Stratton didn't even wait to see who it was. Obviously assuming the new arrival was Griffin, he shot.

Raleigh issued a muffled scream.

This was likely to be Griffin's only chance, and he had to act fast, while Paul still pointed the gun away from Raleigh. In a split second he considered and rejected a number of judo moves, finally opting for a street-fighting all-out body tackle. He launched himself and hit Paul at knee level with the full force of his weight.

Raleigh, who'd been marking Griffin's every movement, was ready. The moment Paul loosened his grip on her, she lunged for his gun hand. All three of them went rolling. Griffin landed on his injured arm, which sent stabbing pain through his whole body, but he had his gun in his other hand, and it was aimed at Paul's head.

Griffin was fractional seconds away from pulling the trigger when he realized Raleigh had come up onto her knees, and she had Paul's gun gripped in her duct-taped hands.

"Everybody freeze. Griffin, don't shoot. We got him."

It took all of Griffin's willpower not to stare at her, but he kept his gaze on their adversary. "Raleigh, are you okay? Where are you hurt?"

During that half moment of distraction, Paul Stratton lunged to his hands and knees, then his feet. He was unarmed now but still dangerous.

"Down on your knees!" Griffin shouted the way he'd heard countless TV cops and a few real ones say. "Hands behind your head."

Paul smiled a bit wildly and refused to obey. "Uh-uh. You think I'm going to let you humiliate me?

Prove everything I wrote about Anthony Simonetti is a lie? That story made me who I am and you—" he pointed at Raleigh "—you were going to take that away from me. And you—" He turned back to Griffin "—you're just a cocky kid, and yet the folks at CNI thought you were my equal. It shouldn't have been a contest. *I won a Pulitzer!* I'm not about to let you take that job from me."

Even after all that had happened, Griffin felt a grain of sadness for Paul Stratton, who was watching his career bleed away and couldn't do anything about it.

"It's over, Paul."

"It's not over until I say it's over." With that, he turned and ran full tilt to the edge of the building and, without hesitation, hurled himself over.

"No!" Raleigh screamed. She ran after Paul, but Griffin headed her off.

"You don't want to look." Paul might survive a three-story fall onto concrete, but chances were the outcome was messy.

As sickened as he was by Paul's cowardly act, he was more worried about Raleigh, covered in blood and pale as death itself.

He took her into his arms. "Where are you hurt, baby?"

"It's just a nosebleed. I'm fine." She pulled out of his attempted embrace. "Paul shot someone. The fire escape. Who was it?"

Celeste. How could Griffin have forgotten? "Stay here." He sprinted to the fire escape and, steeling himself, looked over the edge. Instead of a bloody tragedy, he was met with Celeste climbing up.

"What happened?"

"You're okay? I thought you were shot."

"No, but my hat didn't fare too well. And that balloon is history." She pointed to a crumpled bit of shiny Mylar clinging to the metal stairway railing below.

"Thank God."

"You think I'm dumb enough to stick my head right into the line of fire? I wasn't born yesterday, you know. What happened? You two okay?"

Raleigh had joined them. "We're fine. Thank you, Celeste. Your actions saved my life. And you." She looped her taped wrists around Griffin's head and hugged him. "Thank you for coming after me. Thank you for saving me. I've never been so scared."

"That makes two of us."

"Awww, now that's sweet." Celeste beamed up at them.

## CHAPTER SIXTEEN

"WHAT DO YOU MEAN, you don't want the job?" Pierce Fontaine of CNI demanded. "You won it fair and square."

"Not so hard, when your competition is dead," Griffin pointed out. It was four days since the rooftop showdown, and Griffin was at the *Telegram* office, cleaning out his desk, talking to Pierce Fontaine on his Bluetooth as he emptied drawers.

"But that's the crux of the story," Pierce enthused. "And no one can tell it like you can. You were there, right in the middle of things. I can't even imagine the ratings!"

Was this guy for real? *Ratings?*

"Pierce, I wouldn't write this story for CNI if you were the last news outlet on earth."

"I…I beg your pardon?"

How soon they forget. "You sold me out. You told me I had two weeks. Then you ran with that piece of sensational crap on the basis of one lousy, anonymous phone call."

"It wasn't an anonymous call," Pierce protested.

"Stratton said he was you. We thought we were talking to you! You—Stratton—said to run with it."

"Spin it any way you want," Griffin said. "You still showed gross negligence by slandering Raleigh without even giving her the chance to defend herself. I can't work for such an irresponsible organization."

"But it's nearly a seven-figure salary! You're walking away from that?"

Poor guy just didn't get it. "Yes, Pierce, I'm walking away. Not only that, but if Raleigh sues you, I'll be her star witness." Griffin disconnected the call and, with a shake of his head, resumed his packing.

Even if CNI hadn't made such a monumental screwup, Griffin was pretty sure he wouldn't have taken the job. He didn't want to write the story.

Someone else would take care of that—probably every reporter in the country wanted a crack at it. Griffin had been bombarded with calls from journalists as far away as Uzbekistan, wanting the inside scoop.

Juicy stories used to get him all excited. Now that he was in the middle of a sensational mess, however, he found it not so pleasant. This whole experience had caused him to reevaluate his career aspirations. He loved digging for the truth, loved shining a light on wrongdoing, but he also realized that news reporting had the capacity to harm people. Poor Anthony Simonetti spent years in prison partly due to Paul's overzealous—and inaccurate—reporting.

Maybe it was time for Griffin to dust off that novel he'd half written in college and finish it. He had a little money saved up.

As he loaded the last box onto a hand truck, he checked his watch. Only a half hour until his appointment with Daniel Logan. Daniel hadn't said why he wanted to meet, but Griffin was pretty sure an apology for misjudging him was in the offing. And when a billionaire wanted to apologize, it was best to let him.

"Sure you won't change your mind?" It was Marvin Gussler, his editor. He stood near Griffin's desk, squinting through his thick glasses.

"I can't believe you'd want me to stay," Griffin said. "I was writing something for another news outfit while on your payroll."

Marv shook his head. "You were tempted by a boatload of money. It happens. Doesn't negate all the great stories you've written for us, and the ones you could write in the future."

Griffin thought that was mighty broad-minded of the man. He shook Marv's hand. "If I decide to go back to work as a reporter, I'll talk to you first."

"That's all I can ask."

Exactly thirty minutes later, feeling light and surprisingly optimistic about his unemployed status, Griffin was ushered into Daniel Logan's private office. He wasn't sure what to expect, but he was damn curious.

Daniel was all smiles as he came to his feet. "Griffin. Good of you to come."

"No problem." Griffin shook the man's hand, and they each settled into chairs. Daniel's was some high-tech office model that rolled and spun on a dozen multidirectional casters. Griffin's was an enormous, plush wingback that looked out of place in the high-tech lair.

"First, I want to apologize for jumping to conclusions about your actions, about your character. I should have known better simply on the basis of my association with you. My first impression of you was strongly positive, and I'm rarely wrong in that department. I was an idiot to arrive at the answer I did, and I'm sorry."

Griffin was impressed. Wealthy, powerful men seldom had to apologize for their actions. If they made a mistake, they hired someone to take care of it, or bought their way out somehow.

"I accept your apology. It was a tough, confusing situation. Maybe none of us were at our best."

Daniel smiled. "Good. Glad that's out of the way. Now we can get down to business. I understand you've left your job at the *Telegram*."

How would Daniel Logan know that? The man had ears everywhere. "I need a break from news writing," Griffin said.

"So you haven't accepted a job elsewhere?"

"No." A couple of newspapers and a wire service

had put out feelers, but he hadn't returned their calls. Maybe he would feel differently in a week or two.

"I have a proposition for you, then. How would you like to work for me?"

For a moment, all Griffin could do was stare with his mouth gaping open like a landed fish. "Doing what? Public relations?"

"God, how boring. No, of course not. I want you to work as an investigator at Project Justice."

Of all the scenarios Griffin had imagined, this wasn't one of them. "I thought all of your people were former law enforcement. Or lawyers."

"Right now they are. But you've got the skills I need. You're a good investigator, and you can handle yourself in a tight spot. You've also shown that you're honest and ethical, and you have some knowledge of the law. All of those are qualities I value in my people, and I don't care how you acquired them."

Griffin didn't reply right away. He was sorely tempted, but he'd just been through a life-changing event, which meant it wasn't a good time to make snap decisions. "Can I think about it?"

"Of course. But, for the record, you'd be paid more than you would have earned from CNI."

"Really." He knew Daniel compensated his people well, but he'd had no idea. "You know, there is one problem."

"Do you mean Raleigh?"

"Yeah." He hadn't seen her since that night on

the roof. Once the police had arrived, they'd been separated and questioned for hours. Then Griffin had slept for twelve hours straight.

When he woke, he'd set about rearranging his life. He had called Raleigh and left a message on her cell, letting her know he was thinking about her, but that was as close as he'd gotten to talking to her.

He was in love with Raleigh—he was more sure of that than ever. But he also knew she wasn't ready for a relationship, not the kind he wanted. She might never be.

But he would wait. If and when she *was* ready to love again, he'd be there.

"Raleigh might not feel comfortable working with me day in and day out," Griffin said. "Things between us are complicated."

"How about if I let you two settle that issue yourselves?" Daniel nodded toward the doorway of his office and Griffin turned to find a vision standing there. Raleigh—but not Raleigh. Instead of a boxy suit, she had on a colorful floral sundress that showed off her spectacular figure. She'd ditched the horn-rim glasses. Her ears were adorned with dangly gold earrings with little bells that tinkled with each move of her head.

And her hair—holy cow. No more slicked-back ponytail or matronly bun. Now her hair fell in shimmering auburn waves past her shoulders in an untamed waterfall of fire and autumn leaves.

On her feet, instead of low-heeled pumps, were a pair of gold sandals sporting red silk flowers.

Griffin's mouth went dry. "Uh, hi."

She smiled, looking more relaxed than he'd ever seen her. "Hi, yourself."

Daniel rose and emerged from behind his computer console. "I'll just go see about lunch." Raleigh stepped inside, allowing Daniel to exit.

Griffin stood, unsure what to do now. "I didn't know you'd be here."

"Daniel graciously invited me to stay on a few days so I can…decompress. He insists I continue my 'vacation,' and I guess that's a good idea."

"It *is* a good idea," Griffin agreed. "You don't want to go back to your apartment until the windows are repaired and everything gets cleaned up." He was thinking specifically about the bullet holes all over the place, and the blood he'd smeared on her rugs and furniture.

"Oh, that's all done. Daniel took care of it. I was there last night, in fact, straightening up. Changing a few things." She flashed an enigmatic smile. "So, you've decided not to take the job at CNI?"

"You're kidding, right?"

"Yeah, I guess I am. You're too ethical to work with that sleazy outfit. But you probably have other options."

"Everybody wants the story," he agreed. "But they're not getting it. I'm ready to put this whole thing behind me. It's left a very bad taste in my mouth." He still had trouble wrapping his mind around the fact that a colleague had been willing to commit murder for the sake of his ambition.

Raleigh's forehead wrinkled with a worry line. "Does that mean you want to put me behind you, as well?"

"No," he said bluntly. "I was out of my mind when I tried to cut things off between us. It was because I was scared of my feelings. I've never felt this way about any woman."

He wanted to go to her, take her in his arms, kiss her until she swooned. But he couldn't. Not yet.

"I know you're not ready for that much intensity. I know you're still healing. That's why I didn't give Daniel an answer. Seeing each other every day, working together and not *being* together—it would be tough. For both of us, I think."

"It doesn't have to be like that." She closed the distance between them and took his hand between both of hers. "I have something to show you. Will you come with me?"

"Of course."

Griffin was consumed with curiosity, but he let Raleigh lead the way through the foyer and out to the driveway, where her Volvo was parked. Copper trotted behind them, and soon all three of them were seated inside the car.

"It's nice to be able to drive myself around without

worrying about someone trying to kill me," she said lightly as she started up the engine.

It was nice. The weather was mild, the sun shining. Griffin opened his window. Copper, sitting in his lap, stuck his head out and barked at the wind. Raleigh turned up the radio.

Griffin noticed she was no longer wearing her wedding ring.

"I haven't told you the good news yet," she said. "The police finally got around to running the gun's registration number. Guess who it belonged to?"

"Louis Costanza?"

"You got it. Plus, the missing bullet? It mysteriously showed up."

"Someone in the Houston P.D. has a conscience."

"They've matched the bullets. We have a murder weapon, traced to someone other than Anthony. The governor has stayed Anthony's execution. They're going to reopen the case, and I have high hopes Anthony's conviction will be overturned."

"Congratulations." He was genuinely pleased for her. "But I thought you were on vacation."

"I am. Beth is coordinating the evidence. She's keeping me updated."

"Guess we were wrong about your father-in-law. Have you checked on him lately?"

Raleigh smiled. "John's prognosis is excellent. He's too mean to die. I sent him a big basket of flowers and a card with a huge apology for arguing with him when he was critically ill."

"That was nice."

"Then I called Abe Comstock and told him how the Shinns reacted to the words *Swiss bank account.* Even though they had nothing to do with the money in my account."

"Ooh, not so nice after all."

"I'm done with the Shinns for good. Jason would understand."

They rode in companionable silence. Griffin was happy just to watch the wind play in Raleigh's gorgeous mop of hair.

"I like your hair that way," he said after a while.

"Thanks. It feels nice just to let it go sometimes. I couldn't find a blow dryer this morning. I think Jillian hid it from me. She's been after me to try a different hairstyle."

"And is Jillian behind the, er, wardrobe change?"

Raleigh blushed prettily.

"You do look beautiful. For the record, I like the suits and the bun and the glasses, too. The uptight librarian look turns me on."

"Griffin!"

"It's what first drew me to you. But today…" He couldn't even put into words how hot he was for her. And maybe he shouldn't try.

Raleigh drove downtown, to her apartment building, and into the garage. Griffin, more curious by the minute, followed her to the elevator. What was she up to?

"I just wanted to show you how nicely everything cleaned up," Raleigh said. "I don't know where Daniel gets his people, but they were fast and thorough. If I didn't know, I would never guess what went on here only a few days ago."

She opened her front door with a flourish.

Griffin was impressed. The French doors to the patio had been replaced. The rugs were free of shattered glass. The carpets and upholstery had been cleaned. He picked up a pillow from the sofa, remembering how he had used it to stanch the flow of blood from his arm. It looked immaculate.

In fact, the apartment looked exactly as it had before—no, not exactly. Something was different.

Copper noticed it first. After dashing inside and sniffing at every corner, he trotted to one particular corner of the living room and sniffed all around.

Then Griffin got it. No more shrine. The table with all the photos of Jason and memorabilia was gone, replaced by a potted ficus tree.

"It was time," Raleigh said simply. "Six years is way too long to mourn. I'm ready to move forward."

Griffin was happily stunned. "I wouldn't want you to forget him entirely," he said, surprising himself.

"I couldn't do that. Look, I left one picture on the mantel. See?"

Yes, there was a small, framed picture of Jason, a candid snapshot of him laughing. But other pictures surrounded him—photos of Raleigh's parents, a picture of Beth from Project Justice dressed like a mouse for Halloween, another picture of Copper and an unidentified cat, one of Raleigh at her law school graduation.

When he turned to look at her, her green eyes shone bright with hopefulness.

"I love you, Griffin."

He opened his mouth to respond, but she cut him off.

"Now, I know you might not be ready for that, and that's okay. I don't want that to stand in the way of Daniel's job offer. I can work with you under any circumstances. Even if you tell me that I misunderstood, that we don't have anything special, I can handle it. I'm the strongest person in the world—"

"Raleigh. Stop."

"No, really. It's important that you know that. You don't have to feel uncomfortable around me."

"I don't. I won't. Can I get a word in edgewise?"

"Sorry. I don't usually babble. Guess I'm nervous."

She wasn't the only one. He'd never been in love, never had to tell a woman of his feelings before. *Here goes.*

"I won't feel uncomfortable around you. I love you too, Raleigh. You *are* strong. But you're smart and compassionate and loving and generous. I could never have moved to New York, so far away from you. I was willing to wait until you were ready to love again."

Her eyes filled with tears. "Oh, Griffin."

Enough talk. They would have a lifetime to talk. He pulled her to him and captured her soft, incredible mouth in his and kissed her until he was light-headed and her knees buckled.

"There's one room you haven't shown me," he said, holding his breath. Too much too soon?

Raleigh, clearly beyond words, pointed to a doorway. He swept her up into his arms and carried her toward the bedroom as she issued an uncharacteristic giggle.

"Your apartment looks great, Raleigh. But I think you'll be moving soon. Into a bigger place."

Raleigh sighed and rested her head against his shoulder.

* * * * *

*Daniel Logan spent six years in prison
for a crime he didn't commit,
so he doesn't have a high opinion
of those who work in the judicial system.
But he may have met his match in
prosecuting attorney Jamie McNair!*

*Be sure to look for* A Score to Settle,
*the next book in Kara Lennox's*
PROJECT JUSTICE *miniseries.
Available in April 2011.*

# COMING NEXT MONTH

### Available April 12, 2011

**#1698 RETURN TO THE BLACK HILLS**
*Spotlight on Sentinel Pass*
Debra Salonen

**#1699 THEN THERE WERE THREE**
*Count on a Cop*
Jeanie London

**#1700 A CHANCE IN THE NIGHT**
*Mama Jo's Boys*
Kimberly Van Meter

**#1701 A SCORE TO SETTLE**
*Project Justice*
Kara Lennox

**#1702 BURNING AMBITION**
*The Texas Firefighters*
Amy Knupp

**#1703 DESERVING OF LUKE**
*Going Back*
Tracy Wolff

You can find more information on upcoming
Harlequin® titles, free excerpts and more at
**www.HarlequinInsideRomance.com.**

HSRCNM0311

# REQUEST YOUR FREE BOOKS!
## 2 FREE NOVELS PLUS 2 FREE GIFTS!

**Harlequin®**

*Super Romance®*

### Exciting, emotional, unexpected!

**YES!** Please send me 2 FREE Harlequin® Superromance® novels and my 2 FREE gifts (gifts are worth about $10). After receiving them, if I don't wish to receive any more books, I can return the shipping statement marked "cancel." If I don't cancel, I will receive 6 brand-new novels every month and be billed just $4.69 per book in the U.S. or $5.24 per book in Canada. That's a saving of at least 15% off the cover price! It's quite a bargain! Shipping and handling is just 50¢ per book in the U.S. and 75¢ per book in Canada.* I understand that accepting the 2 free books and gifts places me under no obligation to buy anything. I can always return a shipment and cancel at any time. Even if I never buy another book, the two free books and gifts are mine to keep forever.

135/336 HDN FC6T

Name _____ (PLEASE PRINT)

Address _____ Apt. #

City _____ State/Prov. _____ Zip/Postal Code

Signature (if under 18, a parent or guardian must sign)

Mail to the **Reader Service:**
**IN U.S.A.:** P.O. Box 1867, Buffalo, NY 14240-1867
**IN CANADA:** P.O. Box 609, Fort Erie, Ontario L2A 5X3

Not valid for current subscribers to Harlequin Superromance books.

**Are you a current subscriber to Harlequin Superromance books
and want to receive the larger-print edition?
Call 1-800-873-8635 or visit www.ReaderService.com.**

* Terms and prices subject to change without notice. Prices do not include applicable taxes. Sales tax applicable in N.Y. Canadian residents will be charged applicable taxes. Offer not valid in Quebec. This offer is limited to one order per household. All orders subject to credit approval. Credit or debit balances in a customer's account(s) may be offset by any other outstanding balance owed by or to the customer. Please allow 4 to 6 weeks for delivery. Offer available while quantities last.

**Your Privacy**—The Reader Service is committed to protecting your privacy. Our Privacy Policy is available online at www.ReaderService.com or upon request from the Reader Service.

We make a portion of our mailing list available to reputable third parties that offer products we believe may interest you. If you prefer that we not exchange your name with third parties, or if you wish to clarify or modify your communication preferences, please visit us at www.ReaderService.com/consumerchoice or write to us at Reader Service Preference Service, P.O. Box 9062, Buffalo, NY 14269. Include your complete name and address.

*Selene wanted nothing to do with the father of her son, Alex; but Aristedes had other plans...that included them.*

*Read on for an sneak peek from*
*THE SARANTOS SECRET BABY by Olivia Gates,*
*available April 2011, only from Harlequin Desire.*

"You were right to turn my marriage offer down," Aristedes said.

And Selene found her voice at last, found the words that would not betray the blow he'd dealt her. "Thanks for letting me know. You didn't have to come all the way here, though. You could have just let it go. I left yesterday with the understanding that this case is closed."

Before the hot needles behind her eyes could dissolve into an unforgivable display of stupidity and weakness, she began to close the door.

The door stopped against an immovable object. His flat palm.

"I can't accept that." His voice was low, leashed.

What did her tormentor mean now? Was he ending one game only to start another?

She raised eyes as bruised as her self-respect to his, found nothing there but solemnity and determination.

Before she could voice her confusion, he elaborated. "I never let anything go unless I'm certain it's unworkable. I realize I made you an unworkable offer, and that's why I'm withdrawing it. I'm here to offer something else. A workability study."

She leaned against the door, thankful for its support and partial shield. "Your son and I are not a business venture you can test for feasibility."

His gaze grew deeper, made her feel as if he was trying to delve into her mind, take control of it. "It's actually the other way around. I'm the one who would be tested."

She shook her head. "Why bother? I know—and *you* know—you're not workable. Not with me."

His spectacular eyebrows lowered over eyes she felt were emitting silver hypnosis. "You're right again. Neither you nor I have any reason to believe that isn't the truth. The only truth. It might be best for both you and Alex to never hear from me again, to forget I exist. But then again, maybe not. I'm only asking for the chance for both of us to find out for certain. You believe I'm unworkable in any personal relationship. I've lived my life based on that belief about myself. I never really had reason to question it. But I have one now. In fact, I have two."

*Find out what happens in*
*THE SARANTOS SECRET BABY by Olivia Gates,*
*available April 2011, only from Harlequin Desire.*

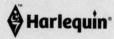

# Harlequin® Romance

# MARGARET WAY

## *In the Australian Billionaire's Arms*

Handsome billionaire David Wainwright isn't about to let his favorite uncle be taken for all he's worth by mysterious and undeniably attractive florist Sonya Erickson.

But David soon discovers that Sonya's no greedy gold digger. And as sparks sizzle between them, will the rugged Australian embrace the secrets of her past so they can have a chance at a future together?

*Don't miss this incredible new tale,*
*available in April 2011*
*wherever books are sold!*

### Harlequin®

## A Romance FOR EVERY MOOD™

www.eHarlequin.com

HR17722